THE
SAGAS
OF
MANN

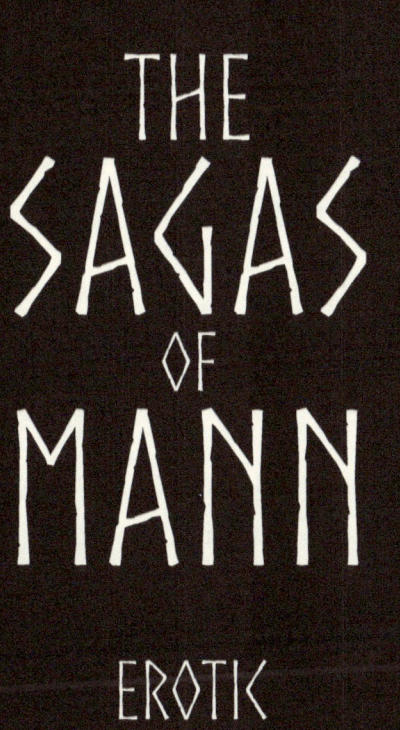

THE SAGAS OF MANN

EROTIC VIKING TALES

JEFF MANN

UNZIPPED

THE SAGAS OF MANN

Erotic Viking Tales by JEFF MANN

Unzipped Books, an imprint of Lethe Press
lethepressbooks.com

Published in the United States of America

Cover and Interior Design by INKSPIRAL DESIGN.

ISBN 978-1-59021-612-5

For

STEVE BERMAN
*with profound thanks for decades
of support, advice, and friendship*

In memory of

MARY RENAULT
and
PATRICIA NELL WARREN

ACKNOWLEDGMENTS

"Loki's Boy" first appeared in *Raising Hell: Demonic Gay Erotica,*
edited by Todd Gregory (Valley Falls, New York: Bold Strokes Books, 2012).

"1066 AD" first appeared in *Lust in Time: Erotic Romance Through the Ages*, edited by Rob Rosen (Albion, New York: MLR Press, 2013).

"Mead-Sweet" first appeared in *Wings: Subversive Gay Angel Erotica,*
edited by Todd Gregory (Valley Falls, New York: Bold Strokes Books, 2011).

"The Saga of Einar and Gisli" first appeared in
On the Run: Tales of Gay Pursuit and Passion, edited by Jerry L. Wheeler (Springfield, Missouri: Wilde City Press, 2014).

CONTENTS

SWORD-SWINGERS
AND
FLESH-SWORDS

I.

THIS AFTERNOON, A BALMY DAY in the last half of April 2023, I finally have time to begin forging a few pages of preparatory notes into an introduction for *The Sagas of Mann: Erotic Viking Tales*. I've left my husband John and our two tabbies at home in Pulaski, Virginia, and have sought writing solitude in my native mountains, in my hometown of Hinton, West Virginia, in the solid house I inherited from my father. Today, contemplating how to explain the genesis of the three short stories and novella contained in this volume of historical fiction, I realize abruptly that the immediate present—what's around me, what's in the mirror—is the perfect place to begin, for it clearly illustrates my passionate interest in the Norse past, an enthusiasm that has spawned these tales.

What's around me? I'm tapping on my laptop in the back parlor while listening to my personalized YouTube mix, soundtracks from the TV series *Vikings* as well as Norse-themed instrumental music by Wardruna, Danheim, Gealdyr, Forndom, and Osi and the Jupiter. I'm drinking coffee from a big black mug that sports a Viking emblem called the Helm of Awe, the runic alphabet called the Elder Futhark, and "BLOOD OF MY ENEMIES" in big red letters. The coffee cup I used yesterday displays the image of a Viking warrior, brandishing a bearded axe and striding towards the sea. About him are printed the words, "You are either on my side, by my side, or in my fucking way. Choose wisely." On an old desk, which doubles as a makeshift home altar, are statues of Odin, Freya, and Baldur, each with a shot-glass offering of liquor, plus a drinking horn, a box of lapis lazuli rune stones, and a tankard with images of Thor and Odin on it. By the CD player is a small replica of a Viking-Age dragon-headed ship that serves as a candleholder for tea lights, as well as a nutcracker in the shape of a Viking warrior, a red-bearded little guy complete with helmet, upraised sword, and shield. On a corner table is a statue of Thor lunging forward, wielding a huge hammer, another shot-glass offering before him.

What's in the mirror? An eccentric oddity! A Viking wannabe! My head's shaved (the best way by far to deal with male pattern baldness). My salt-and-pepper beard is long and bushy, nearly down to my navel, the tip adorned with a small metal Thor's-hammer beard ring. Today's T-shirt is green camo, sporting another Elder-Futhark ring, another Helm of Awe, and "Berserker" in big white letters. Among my myriad tattoos are a Thor's hammer; the Triple Horn of Odin; The Helm of Awe surrounded by Odin's ravens, Huginn and Muninn; a flaming sword; a shield crossed by four spears; and the rune Tiwaz, meaning "warrior." On my right ring finger is a black ring inscribed with the Valknut, and around my right wrist is a Viking arm ring with bear heads, crafted in Ukraine, once the home of the Rus, Swedish traders during the Viking Age.

A lot of past reading and traveling has crafted this peculiar present. I often jokingly refer to myself as "The Hillbilly Heathen" (said phrase serving as the title of the introduction to the 2020 illustrated re-release of my 2011 poetry collection, *Ash: Poems from Norse Mythology*). Though I'd encountered Norse myth in my youth, thanks to Marvel Comics and Edith Hamilton's *Mythology*, it wasn't until I began reading primary Norse sources in Spring 2003 that I became truly hooked. Sitting in on a graduate independent study class on Norse and Celtic literature at Virginia Tech, where I've taught since 1989, I devoured *The Poetic Edda*, *The Prose Edda*, and a goodly number of Icelandic sagas, including *Egil's Saga*, *Grettir's Saga*, *Laxardal Saga*, and *The Saga of the Volsungs*. Since then, I've revisited much of that material and read many other sagas, as well as piles of nonfiction books about Norse mythology and the Viking Age. I've also twice co-taught "Old Norse Literature: Land into Legend" at Virginia Tech and taken students to Iceland for Study Abroad trips, where we cautiously strolled black-sand beaches, climbed glaciers, visited volcanic mud-pots, crept inside ice caves, and visited museums dedicated to the sagas.

Part of the attraction has been Viking religion. A neopagan from way back, I've become deeply dedicated to Asatru/Heathenry, the modern reconstruction of Norse spirituality. Another appeal has been the Viking value system, which has many parallels in my own Appalachian upbringing. Along with attachment to clan and land (and an inconvenient longing for blood-revenge, I must admit), the "Nine Heathen Virtues" espoused by contemporary Heathenism make perfect sense to this mountain man: Courage, Truth, Honor, Fidelity, Discipline, Hospitality, Self-Reliance, Industriousness, and Perseverance.

Opportunities to compose my own Viking-themed fiction came along starting in 2010, thanks to editors' invitations or calls for submission. "Mead-Sweet" appeared first, in Todd Gregory's 2011 *Wings: Subversive Gay Angel Erotica*, followed by "Loki's Boy" in Gregory's 2012 companion volume, *Raising Hell: Demonic Gay Erotica*, then "1066 AD" in Rob Rosen's 2013 *Lust in Time: Erotic Romance Through the Ages*. Finally, "The Saga of Einar and Gisli" was one of four novellas included in Jerry L. Wheeler's 2014 *On the Run: Tales of Gay Pursuit and Passion*. For reasons that will become obvious, in this present collection I haven't arranged the tales in the order in which they were written.

"Loki's Boy" was inspired by Snorri Sturluson's *Prose Edda*. In the *Gylfaginning* section, he tells the now-well-known story of Baldur's death, including Loki's culpability and punishment. In *Gylfaginning*, Snorri also describes the final battle between the gods and the giants during Ragnarök. Loki, like all the tricksters of global mythology, and like untamed erotic energy in general, is a breaker of rules, social constructs, order, and expectations, so it seems to me that transgressive sexuality like BDSM would appeal to him. I suspect I had Chris Hemsworth's handsome looks in mind for this story's protagonist, since I'm a fan of Hemsworth in Marvel's *Thor* films. If I were Loki, I too would collect a harem, and if I were Loki, I too would keep them around both to ravish with regularity and to marshal against my enemies. (Writing fiction certainly has its vicarious satisfactions. In my case, it's a way to safely channel and release my painfully trammeled lust and rage.)

As for the companion tales "1066 AD" and "Mead-Sweet," though I wrote "Mead-Sweet" first, in terms of narrative chronology "1066 AD" comes first. In that short story, I created a prequel for "Mead-Sweet," envisioning Thorir and Eirik's relationship in Midgard and the details of their separation. In order to write the last scene, when the rune *Wunjo* appears, I further researched the Elder Futhark. My fascination with Norse runes began with the composition of the *Ash* poems in 2003-2004 and has only deepened over the years. In fact, during the summer of 2020 I composed an entire MS of poetry, as yet unpublished, writing three poems for each of the twenty-four runes.

A battle often regarded as the end of the Viking Age stirred me to write "Mead-Sweet." To borrow from Wikipedia's entry for "Battle of Stamford Bridge":

> The sudden appearance of the English army caught the Norwegians by surprise. The English advance was then delayed by the need to pass through the choke-point presented by the bridge itself. The Anglo-Saxon Chronicle has it that a giant Norse axeman (possibly armed with a Dane Axe) blocked the narrow crossing

and single-handedly held up the entire English army. The story is that this axeman cut down up to 40 Englishmen and was defeated only when an English soldier floated under the bridge in a half-barrel and thrust his spear through the planks in the bridge, mortally wounding the axeman.

Another useful source for this story was Snorri's *Prose Edda* yet again. In *Gylfaginning*, he describes Valhalla, "The Hall of the Slain," in some detail: the great size of the hall, the presence of Odin, the throng of *einherjar* (those who've died in battle), the fighting all day and the feasting all night on mead and boar-meat. I thought a pleasing gay take on the Norse afterlife would include lots of vigorous warrior-on-warrior fucking after all the fighting and feasting, and, as someone with a vengeful streak a mile wide, the thought of spending eternity dismembering those I despise appeals to me a great deal. So, more fiction as wish-fulfillment. I also thought it would be an interesting change of pace to create a male Valkyrie, "the Choosers of the Slain," moved as I was by depictions of them in *The Poetic Edda, The Prose Edda,* and a few sagas.

Both "1066 AD" and "Mead-Sweet" are informed by a particular erotic conflict, one based on Norse society's contempt for men who play the passive role in anal intercourse, what some might today call "bottom-shaming." Having had a lifelong fascination with/craving for butch bottoms—and often serving as one myself—in these two stories and in the novella that follows, I explore the contrast between traditional masculinity—with its focus on independence, power, and strength (a version of manhood I grew up around in rural and small-town Appalachia and have adopted to a great extent)—and the perverse pleasures of surrender and powerlessness in BDSM relationships, where the butch bottom gives up masculine dominance and revels in masculine submission. Sword-swingers who sometimes savor submitting to flesh-swords, in other words.

As for "The Saga of Einar and Gisli," it continues the focus on masculine men who take erotic pleasure in bottoming, however much shame that might evoke in them. The novella explores how that shame can make a man fearful, vengeful, hypocritical, destructive, and treacherous, until he finally finds the strength and understanding to be proud of who he really is and what he really wants. Gisli's name is borrowed from that of the heroic outlaw in *Gisli Sursson's Saga*, and his looks, I must lustily confess, are based on those of a young man I used to admire two decades ago. A fellow member of The Weight Club, a gym I used to frequent in Blacksburg, Virginia, he was featured earlier in an essay of mine, "Valhalla in the Redwoods," published first in *Chiron Review* (2005) and later in *Binding the God: Ursine Essays from the Mountain South* (2010). In the aesthete's mind, beauty lingers, however distant in place or time.

Many Icelandic sagas include poetry within the prose tale, a good example being *Egil's Saga*, which often features the warrior-poet protagonist "speaking a verse," so I thought it might pleasing to sprinkle "The Saga of Einar and Gisli" with a handful of poems. The romantic setting of Freysholm is based to some extent on the remote island of Drangey, where the titular outlaw takes refuge in *The Saga of Grettir the Strong*. The temple of Frey near the novella's end is based on the famed Temple of Uppsala, described by Adam of Bremen in his *History of the Archbishops of Hamburg-Bremen*; Frey's penchant for freeing prisoners is mentioned in *The Poetic Edda*. As for the scorn-pole effigies that Gisli constructs, erecting such public insults was a real practice, described in some detail in *Egil's Saga*, Chapter 58, and Chapter 2 of *Gisli Sursson's Saga*. The novella's final setting—the Orkney Islands—I chose because of its Norse history—detailed in *Orkneyinga Saga: The History of the Earls of Orkney*—and because of my fondness for its beauty. My husband's father's family hailed from there many generations ago, and in 2013, John and I spent over a week on Mainland Orkney, relishing its quiet meadows, its Neolithic ruins and stone circles, its Scotch and beer, and its sea-side cliffs. The past, both prehistoric and Norse, was hauntingly palpable.

II.

Today, the second day of this essay's composition, I'm wearing a black T-shirt purchased online from my favorite Viking-themed company, Grimfrost in Sweden. White letters across my chest proclaim: "Fight

All Day, Feast All Night. Einherjar Live Forever." Before heading over here to West Virginia, I'd packed this T-shirt without much thought. Only this morning I'm realizing the odd synchronicity, to be wearing such a garment the day after summarizing Snorri's descriptions of Valhalla in *Gylfaginning*.

Forty-five years ago, I was a teenager in this house, newly aware of my same-sex attractions and trying to make sense of them. Some of the validation I needed I got from lesbian friends. Some I got from gay-themed fiction, starting with Patricia Nell Warren's novels *The Front Runner* (1974) and *The Fancy Dancer* (1976), and moving on to those of Mary Renault. Renault's depictions of men loving men in ancient Greece—in such novels as *The Last of the Wine* (1956), *Fire from Heaven* (1969), and *The Persian Boy* (1972)— sparked in me a love of history and historical fiction and also gave me much-needed role models, helping me understand how to be a man attracted to other men. Her fictions made vividly clear that homosexual desire has always existed, over millennia, in other places and times, which was a bracing and welcome message.

Later, in college at West Virginia University, I was to discover wonderful gay authors like Felice Picano, Edmund White, Andrew Holleran, and John Rechy. During my high-school years, however, Renault's and Warren's books were the ones I found live-saving, life-changing, spiritually and emotionally nutritive. They gave me what folks today refer to as "representation": literary mirrors in which I might perceive myself and those like me.

For years, I've tried to do the same as Warren and Renault, creating novels in which gay men might see themselves, whether in the present—in my novels *Cub* (2014) and *Country* (2016)—or in the past—in my Civil War fiction, *Purgatory* (2012*)*, *Salvation* (2014), and "Camp Allegheny" (2011). Here in *The Sagas of Mann*, I've attempted something similar, this time using the Viking Age as the setting for gay desire. I truly hope this collection of Norse-themed tales lends readers some of the encouragement, validation and reflection I've received from fiction. Existence can be difficult, especially for minorities, but artistic affirmations can help us survive.

LOKI'S
BOY

I T'S HIGH NOON BY THE time Gunnar reaches the pool. Sweating and panting after the long ascent, he pulls off his musky tunic and wipes his brow and chest with it. He's kicked off his boots and has his trousers peeled down to his knees, ready for a long swim and a sun-soaked nap, when he pauses, full of the sudden conviction that he's being watched.

Not likely in a place so remote, this Norwegian mountainside. The Viking has walked, then climbed, for a good hour, up through his father's highest pastures, where cattle crop summer's lushness, on up through thick woods, then into the high fells, with their windswept grasses and broken rocks, to find this pool where he used to swim as a child. The sun's bright, the sky a pale blue; the breeze is cool on his bare skin. Wary, he scans the dell, seeing no one, hearing nothing but altitudinous air whistling in his ears and the burble of the waterfall descending into the broad pool at its base. Then, reassured that he's indeed alone, he strips off the rest of his garments and dives into the water.

It's colder than he expected. Gunnar shoots to the surface, gasping and laughing, his nipples hard and his genitals shrunken tight with the shock. Still, the water feels good, dulling the ache that lingers in his leg. The dagger wound he received during the last raid on Ireland has healed, leaving a white scar along his blond-furred thigh, but still the limb hurts, and still he limps. Every time it aches, he curses silently, not because the pain is sharp—it's subsided after so many months to a dull throb—but because it's a reminder that he's home, not out on the seas with his Viking companions, achieving booty and glory. He's only twenty-five, but already his reputation as a warrior has waxed large. Another season of inactivity, and who knows what younger, stronger man might supplant him in the people's praises?

Gunnar's come here to escape these thoughts, not mull over them. He tosses mussed locks of hair from his eyes and dives again. After a few strenuous laps about the pool, he climbs onto mossy-slick rocks behind the waterfall and leans into the powerful stream. The sensation's like a strong man's hands massaging his shoulders. Another half an hour of swimming and floating, and, weary at last, he hauls himself from the chilly mere and stretches out on the grass.

The boy's glorious to behold, though he doesn't know it. His thick beard is golden, his long, shaggy hair the pale yellow of mountain dawn. The exertions of farming and battle have sculpted his form into something approaching the ideal: broad shoulders, muscle-thick arms, pectorals swollen with strength. His nipples are large and pink, his chest smooth and white, his belly flat and sprinkled with fine golden hair. Due to these physical blessings, his reputation for fine looks almost equals his reputation for martial prowess. The attentions of farm girls up and down the fjord—Astrid, Ingrid, Gudrun, and Hilde—are numerous and enthusiastic, but he doesn't feel for women what his comrades do, and despite his widowed father's frequent pleas that he marry, so far Gunnar has avoided such entanglements, preferring the companionship of other warriors during the summer raiding parties and the comfort of his father's hearth during the long and bitter winters.

Were he entirely honest with himself, he would realize that the brawny bodies of his Viking shipmates fascinate him far more than the buxom charms of local lasses. Sometimes Gunnar wakes from dreams both confusing and disturbing, in which he's caressing Thorir's red beard or lying beneath Bjorn's strapping weight or even kissing his blood brother Olaf. From these visions, Gunnar wakes gasping and trembling, his belly spattered with his own seed. He knows better than to discuss such dreams with anyone. In Norse society, to accuse a man of desiring another man, of opening his body to another man's thrusting, is one of the gravest insults. Gunnar has no desire to become a pariah, an outlaw. And so he keeps his secret, smiling shyly at the admiration of women, relishing male companionship and the few touches—quick hugs, backslaps, hearty handshakes, shoulder punches—that he can steal during long sea voyages.

His months as an invalid, recovering on his father's fjord-side farm, have denied him those opportunities for physical contact, however, and today, as he lies in the grass, naked and drowsy, the summer sun burnishing his pale skin, the ache for touch vies in intensity with the throbbing of his scarred thigh. If only he were like other men, he thinks, resting a forearm over his eyes. Then he would have a wife and children to come home to after the summer raiding. "Allfather," he whispers, "let me somehow be less lonely." He takes his cock in his hand, gives it a few wistful strokes, and falls asleep.

What wakes him is the same feeling that flooded him when he first reached the banks of the pool: that conviction that someone is watching. Gunnar rubs his eyes and sits up. From the pile of cast-off clothing, he pulls his knife. Unsheathing it, he stands, eyes raking the dell. The sun is low in the sky. Again, there is no one in sight. But this time there is something more to hear than the high winds and the waterfall. Somewhere nearby is a low cry, an animal's.

Gunnar knows that sound. He's heard it back home. It's the raspy caterwaul of a tomcat searching for a she-cat to mount. It sounds again, closer, and then the animal appears by the pond only a few yards away, slinking through wind-restive grass. It hops onto a rock edging the water and regards Gunnar with a green-gold stare.

The animal's deep black, like night sky over sea once a dragon-keeled warship has sailed far from land's small flickers of lamp-gleam and firelight. Yet it glistens, as if its coat were sprinkled with specks of stars. It's large, the largest cat Gunnar has ever seen. It rests on its haunches, laps a paw with a pink tongue, and resumes its intent gaze. It licks its lips and studies his nakedness the way a human being would. It opens its mouth, revealing the tips of white fangs, and snuffles the air, as if savoring Gunnar's scent.

"Here, cat. Here, cat." Gunnar sheaths his knife and pats his sinewy thigh. His farm upbringing has made him fond of animals. He's especially fond of felines. He likes touching them, being touched by them, their soft coats, the way they nestle against him during endless winter nights. It's warmth uncomplicated by human custom or desire, free of risk or judgment. From his clothes, he fetches a leather sack, removing the cloth-wrapped chunk of crumbly white cheese he's brought for a snack. "Here, cat," he coaxes, holding up a piece between thumb and forefinger.

The animal seems unmoved by the offer. Instead, it winks one bright eye, then turns and disappears into the grass.

Why does Gunnar follow? It doesn't occur to him to wonder that. He simply does, leaving his clothes and knife behind. He chews on bites of cheese and limps after the black cat, around the far side of the pool. The sleek animal pauses on a rock ledge, as if it were admiring the great vista below—the steep slope of mountainside, the belts of spruce forest, the pastures of Gunnar's family farm below, the sheer sides of the fjord, and, beyond all that, the open sea. Then it slips over the rock's edge and vanishes.

By the time Gunnar becomes aware of the fact that his bare feet are bleeding, the cat's nowhere to be seen, the cheese is finished, the sun is setting, and the surrounding forest is a thick, shadowy green. He stops, wipes blood off his feet, looks around him, and curses himself for a fool. He's spent his life exploring this mountain, yet somehow he doesn't know where he is. He turns, planning to retrace the path that brought him here, but there is no path, only a thicket of brambles.

No knife, no boots, no clothes, and summer dusk falling fast. His scarred thigh aches. He has no choice but to follow the narrow trail before him, which now takes on green phosphorescence as nightfall nears.

He limps on, feet paining him more and more deeply. Long minutes pass; the darkness completes itself. Gunnar grows more anxious, and thankful that there is no one here to see his folly. With the sun's departure, the mountain air grows cold, and Gunnar's skin pricks with goose pimples.

There, a flickering. Just ahead. A lamplit window, perhaps, a farmstead where he might find aid, shelter and warmth. He moves forward, praying it's no illusion, no will-o'-the-wisp, hoping that no women are there to behold his shameful nakedness.

Soughing trees press in, their soft needles brushing his chest and shoulders. There's the cat, just ahead, its eyes glowing like twinned green mirrors. It caterwauls again, then turns, leading Gunnar farther into the forest, closer to the flickering light.

The path ends at the thorny base of a cliff. To Gunnar's left, dwarfed birches cling to stone; to his right, the land drops off into dim nothingness and the distant roar of cataracts. Before him, beyond a wall of thorns, light gleams from a great crack in the stone. It's a cave.

The cat stops before the thorns, silhouetted by the yellow light, and at last Gunnar catches up to it. It winds itself about his ankles—the sudden silky feel of it causes Gunnar to shudder—then slithers through the bramble-hedge and down a narrow rock-walled passage leading into the earth.

Gunnar hesitates, unsure if he should continue. But a rack of clouds has concealed the summer stars, and a cold breeze has come up, ruffling his long hair and tickling the fine fur between his buttocks. Behind him, the forest's pitch-black. The only light left on earth, as far as his senses are concerned, is that gleaming inside the rock.

"Damn thorns," Gunnar mutters, surveying their hostile points. There's nothing to do but push on through. He's a warrior; he's suffered many wounds. A few pinpricks shan't hurt him. He grits his teeth, closes his eyes, and shoulders into the thicket. The sharp points make his white skin bloom, tiny rosebuds bursting open on the hard curves of his chest, furrows dripping along his narrow hips. One needle catches the tip of his cock and he yelps, cupping his wounded sex in his hands. By the time he's forced his body through, his nakedness is scored, a study in snow and scarlet. Free of the brambles, he pauses, cursing again, impatiently smearing the blood across his chest, arms, and brow.

Warm air courses over him. He staggers into the cave's maw, limping down a long hallway that looks less natural than carved by human tools. The light waxes; he hears the crackle of a fire. The tunnel takes a sharp angle, and then opens up.

Gunnar gapes on the threshold. What enchantment is this? The cave has become a great hall, its walls hung with tapestries, its lofty ceiling disappearing into arched darkness and high windows full of moonlight, moonlight that falls in silvery slants throughout the room. At the far end, a huge hearth is cut into stone, and there a fire blazes. Before it is a wide bed, heaped with blankets and furs. And on that bed, his head propped on pillows, is a man, lounging in a pool of moonlight. He's dark-haired, dark-bearded, and he's naked. His eyes regard Gunnar steadily. His eyes are the cat's, glowing gold-green.

Gunnar, for no reason that he can understand, is afraid. If only he had the knife he left by the pool, or his sword, arrows and bow, all left at home. Nevertheless, a warrior's instinct in the face of fear is to move forward, not back, and so the young Norseman takes another step into the hall. He catches his toe on a stone; simultaneously, the dark man gives a sharp laugh. Gunnar falls onto his hands and knees with a pained gasp. Brief anguish shoots through him; he shakes his head, clearing it.

"It is right that you should kneel." The voice is deep, imperious, and amused. "Stay on your knees, serf, and come to me."

Gunnar gives a low growl. "I am no serf. I am a warrior. I kneel to no one." And even as he says this—a Viking's proud, habitual defiance—he finds himself crawling amazed on hands and knees across the cave's polished floor. Something unseen compels him, invisible and irresistible as wind trembling summer grain or swaying the soughing boughs of snow-coated evergreens.

Gunnar finds himself kneeling beside the bed, his head lowered, his hands clasped behind his back, a position he somehow senses is demanded of him. "Had you a good swim, boy?" the man says, gazing down at Gunnar. "I did enjoy watching you."

"Yes, Lord," Gunnar replies. The reverence in his own voice astounds him, yet reverence seems somehow natural, entirely called for. Gunnar has heard the tales, of gods who appear in human guise to mortal men, Thor and Odin and Loki, gods whose favor or anger makes the difference between life and death. He's heard the tales of sorcery, unnatural powers that rob a man—even a Viking hero—of will. He would resist if he could, but he cannot. Oddly, his own submission feels manly, glorious.

The man swings off the side of the bed and looms over Gunnar. He's a good foot taller than the young Norseman, a good ten years older. Glossy black hair cascades over his shoulders. His cheekbones are sharp, his beard close-cropped, his forehead smooth and high. He's muscular, though less burly than Gunnar, more lithe. His body's coated with black hair, from the pit of his neck to his ankles. His cock's hard, swaying before him like a serpent. It's longer and thicker than Gunnar's, larger than any sex he's furtively studied while bathing with his fellows. A drop of clear moisture glistens at its tip, like rain pendant on birch twigs after a storm.

The stranger smiles, a gleam of white, the lips a satiric curl. He gives Gunnar an emerald wink. "You braved the rose brambles for me." With one hand, the man cups Gunnar's chin. With the other, he dabs blood from Gunnar's thorn-torn brow and licks it off his fingers. "Do you like my looks, serf?"

Gunnar stares up at the stranger's face and powerful torso. Gunnar stares at the stranger's member, which smells of musk and smoke. Gunnar licks his lips and nods. He's never before felt such abject depths of desire. "Yes, Lord," he whispers, throat dry and tight. His own cock hardens, lifting from his thigh and into the air.

"You may," says the stranger. Gunnar nods again, entirely entranced. He shuffles closer, wraps his arms around the man's waist, and shyly licks the tip of his cock. He harvests that clear droplet, savoring its saltiness. Again, his own actions astound him. In dream, perhaps, visions of the night carefully suppressed come the day, he has done such a thing, but never in reality.

The man chuckles. He eases the head of his sex between the boy's lips. Then, seizing him by his shaggy hair, he shoves the stiff member down his throat. Gunnar chokes and sucks and sobs; the man's groin hair tickles his nose; the man's swollen rod batters his gullet till Gunnar's beard is dripping with drool.

Now the man's rhythmic thrusts grow more violent, his grip on Gunnar's hair tightens painfully, and he heaves a guttural groan. Syrupy bitterness fills the Norseman's mouth, the taste a melding of mead, blood, smoke, and cream. His limbs lose all strength, a burning courses through his vitals, darkness slips a soft hood over his head. Gasping for breath, Gunnar slides from sense.

Softness brushes his cheek. Like a cat's fur. Like the face of a god.

Gunnar opens his eyes. He's sprawled upon his own bed. Beside him, his clothes are neatly folded. On the wall, his sheathed knife is hung. The ache in his scarred thigh has spread overnight to all his joints. Stiffly, he tugs on his trousers, climbs from the bed-closet, and limps to the longhouse door. The sun is just rising over the mountain, stretching a path of glitter over the waters of the fjord. In its light, Gunnar can clearly see the myriad thin wounds left by last night's thorns.

"Not a dream? Not a dream." Gunnar runs a hand over the scratched mounds of his chest and shakes his head.

He spends the day shambling from chore to chore about the farm, trying to piece together the mystery of the previous night but only growing more mystified. His father—slender, stooped, gray-bearded, perpetually irascible—berates him every time he passes. "Staggering in after midnight, face bloody! Where were you? What mischiefs did you commit? Drinking! Whoring! Thank the gods your mother didn't live to see such a sight! Your sloth's made you weak. It's robbed you of honor!" At day's end, Gunnar watches the sun set into the sea, takes little nourishment come supper, and retires early.

He wakes to blackness. He's lying on his side. A thick scent pervades the room. It's the smoky musk that filled his nose in last night's vision, the scent of the stranger's naked virility. Now a weight's added to the bed, as if someone unseen had climbed upon it, and fingers brush

Gunnar's hair. The darkness about him is dusted with light, as if star-shine could be mill-ground into meal, golden as the flying pollen of pines. Now someone tickles his thickened sex and strokes its slit. When he groans, a hand grips his jaw, sealing his mouth shut. A voice sounds inside his skull, speaking not a word but the rising inflection of a question. When Gunnar nods, fingers flick his nipples, and then a moistened digit burrows between his buttocks and probes the virgin opening there. Against that invisible palm, Gunnar groans softly and nods again. A fist tightens on his member; the finger between his arse-cheeks digs deeper; hands knead his buttocks; the fingers upon his nipples grow rougher; someone sucks hard on his cock-head. It's as if he were surrounded by, being pleasured by, a multitude of lovers. In another minute, Gunnar's shot his seed into the bedclothes with a stifled shout and has fallen into a sleep deeper than he's known in months.

THE DAYS GROW SHORTER; THE brief Norwegian summer declines. Gunnar's mysterious master—for so Gunnar has come to think of him—comes nearly every week, and always when the boy's alone: in his bed at night, in the stable at twilight, at the mountainside pool at high noon. Sometimes he comes unseen, as that pressure of a strong hand silencing Gunnar's moans, that skillful flicking and kneading of Gunnar's breast and stroking of his sex, the thickness of a finger pushed into his arse, deeper each time, one finger joined by a second and a third, slick with oil, easing the boy open, causing him to buck and writhe with delight, rapture like the vines of bursting roses intertwining his limbs, climbing up the ladder of his spine. Sometimes his master is visible, the same lithe, hairy stranger first met in the mountain cave, lying upon Gunnar and coaxing his body into shuddering, gushing ecstasy. Afterwards, Gunnar comes to consciousness alone, in his bed, in the grass, in the straw of the stable, seed staining his trousers, hands weak and shaking, heart and groin already aching for his master's next visitation.

By autumn's advance, Gunnar's leaner, his golden-furred belly flatter. Food and drink are of no consequence when compared to the delight he finds alone with that unnamed eldritch presence. His thigh no longer throbs, as if his master's touch has healed him. Doing his chores—gathering in hay and firewood, caring for the livestock—he's efficient but distracted. At neighborhood gatherings, he keeps to himself, sipping *gløgg* and staring into the flames. He puts less and less energy into being cordial to the local girls who flirt with him. He doesn't think of the coming winter months, whittling near the long fire and polishing his weapons; he doesn't think of the summer to come, and the raiding parties he might join. His mind is on his master.

THE THORNS TEAR AT HIM again, but he pushes through as he did before. The black cat appeared on his windowsill; he followed it here, through the brisk October day, up the mountainside, through golden aspens, up past the waterfall and into the spruce. Before the bramble-hedge, he stripped. Now, bloodied, he enters the cave. He falls onto his hands and knees and crawls across the floor. His master, naked as well, is standing by the great hearth's blaze. Unbidden, Gunnar drops onto his elbows and kisses the man's feet.

"Why have you come, slave?" The deep voice is dark silk, draping his senses.

"Please, Lord. All. Give me all of you."

His master chuckles. When he nudges Gunnar's mouth with his big toe, the blond Viking takes it into his mouth and begins a gentle sucking.

"All? Are you entirely certain you're ready?"

"Yes, Lord, please. I am ready."

"Are you begging me, boy?"

"I'm begging you, Lord."

"And what will you give me in return? Rings of red-gold? Odin's eight-legged mare?"

"Would that I could, Lord," Gunnar mumbles around the toe. "My body, my devotion, my love are all that—"

His words are cut short as his master wedges the remainder of his toes into Gunnar's mouth, stuffing him full. Gunnar's response is a groan of abject pleasure. He sucks harder. When he feels a hand stroking and squeezing his buttocks, he nods and sucks harder still.

Where did this longing come from, Gunnar wonders idly, as his master removes his foot from Gunnar's reverent mouth, pats the boy's head, then steps behind him, drops to his knees, parts his buttocks, and begins again that maddening, rapturous, oily finger-burrowing. Where and when rose this yearning to be penetrated there, in that fuzzy private place no one sees? Any manly Viking would reject such a desire as base and womanish. But his Lord's commands are loud inside his skull, and the world's an entirely different place when Gunnar's frame is glamoured by the dark man's touch. So Gunnar, on elbows and knees, lowers his cheek to the cold floor, spreads his furry thighs, and lifts his buttocks to his Lord like an offering of gold and ivory. The greasy fingers inside him make him feel strong, young, and loved.

His master's thick cock enters Gunnar roughly, in a rush, shattering the boy's hazy glow of contentment. Anguish envelops him; the Norseman shouts and struggles. Laughing, his Lord seizes Gunnar in his arms and impales him more deeply still. Gunnar pleads, whimpers, and writhes, muscles straining frantically inside his master's imprisoning embrace. "Oh, Lord, no! Please! Oh, it hurts. It hurts!"

"This is good, yes? Oh, so sweet. Have you not dreamed of this since first we met?" Teeth chew Gunnar's ear; a hand brushes tangled locks from his brow. Despite the pain evoked by that hard column of flesh jammed inside him, Gunnar nods.

"You want more, despite the pain." It is not a question, but a statement of fact.

Gunnar moans. His eyes brim with tears. He nods. He shifts his rear, bumping back against his master's loins. The great cock pulls out only to slide slowly in again.

"You will endure agonies for me," whispers the bass voice that months of secret assignations have taught Gunnar to adore. "Willingly. Will you not?"

Without hesitation, Gunnar nods.

"And, come the End, you will battle in my name." Another deep laugh, another painful jabbing of the huge prick, and suddenly Gunnar's released, only to be jerked upright by his thick hair. His master slaps his face and hurls him onto the bed with such rapidity and ease that Gunnar could be the most emaciated of beggars rather than the brawny Norseman he is.

"Let us now prepare you," the dark man says, snapping his fingers. The hearth-fire leaps and crackles; a green sparkling fills the chamber. Whatever enchantment has ensured Gunnar's continued submission now forges bonds that wrap and trap the boy. From beneath the bed flash barbed vines, as if a clambering rose had become sentient, or a sea kraken had lent Gunnar's master the use of its tentacles. In seconds, those spiky vines have bound Gunnar's wrists behind him and snaked about his thick chest and arms. The boy thrashes and screams; the vines grow tighter and tighter; the tiny rose-fangs dig deeper and deeper. "Ah, my God," Gunnar gasps against clenched teeth, trying to be brave. The more violently he flexes against his bonds, the more savagely taut they grow.

His Lord is atop him now, straddling his chest. A finger runs along Gunnar's wet cheek, then trails his upper lip. As if in response to that gesture, thorny strands slither around the lad's head, sink between his teeth, and gag-muffle his moans. Rose-barbs bloody his tongue, his lips, the corners of his mouth.

"What a fine slave you are," says his master, bending to lick tears from the youth's cheek and blood from his lips. The man's hungry mouth moves lower, savaging the boy's chest. His teeth seem sharper and sharper, more an animal's fangs now, gnawing Gunnar's big pink nipples, tearing at his golden-furred belly, sucking and chewing his throbbingly hard sex.

Now, to Gunnar's wonder, the Lord sits astride his prisoner's groin, grips the boy's member, and, with a bass chuckle, lowers himself onto the flesh-seax. Gunnar gasps. Never has he felt such ecstasy.

"Ahhhh, yes," Gunnar's captor groans, rocking and hissing, moving the tight heat of his nether-gate up and down the boy's cock while he tugs and twists the Norseman's bloody nipples and scores his breast and belly with sharp nails.

"So white," the master mutters. "White as sunlit snow. Like my brother-god Baldur." A shadow crosses his face, a second in which triumphant delight wavers. Then he takes his own cock in his hand, and, with a few brief strokes, shoots his seed over Gunnar's face. White lava spatters the Viking's brow and beard with sharp fire.

So spent, a mortal man would soften and drowse. Instead, the Lord slaps the boy's cheek with his prick, which, to Gunnar's amazement, is harder and larger than before.

"Your hole again, serf?"

Gunnar stares at the unsated sex, trembles and nods.

"Yes, God. Please, God." Gunnar musters a muted mumble.

With a chuckle, the Lord heaves Gunnar onto his belly. Sheathing his great cock in the young warrior's arse, he wraps an arm around his throat, clamps a hand over his thorn-gagged mouth, and pounds him into unconsciousness.

NOW IT IS NEVER ENOUGH. Would that Gunnar's master would come every night. But he does not. Instead, his visits become less frequent. During the day, Gunnar works, ignoring his father's nagging. During the night, he curls in bed, burning one moment, shivering the next, stroking himself, fingering his own hole, trying not to cry and most often failing in that attempt. Autumn's yellow leaves fall—the birch, the aspen—torn off by stiffening mountain winds. The pool at the base of the waterfall ices over. Gunnar visits that dell often, hoping to glimpse the black cat. He tromps through evergreens, looking without success for the bramble-hedge and the cave, the hearth-fire and his Lord's warm bed.

He would waste away, for he has little appetite, but he does not. Instead, he forces himself to cook and eat meals he shares with his father by the fire—fish, meat, bread, cheese, ale. His muscled frame is what drew his master to him; somehow he senses that. He keeps himself strong; he salves the fading wounds his Lord's thorny bonds and rough teeth left and aches to be bloodied, wounded, and pierced again. After Winter Nights, he abandons his bed-closet in the family longhouse and moves into a tiny outbuilding, spending his nights private beside a fitful fire, wrapped in blankets and furs, waiting for love's return. He roams the countryside, full of hope, searching for the black cat, restless wanderings his father calls pointless, inexcusable loafing.

And when at long last that smoky musk fills his nostrils—in his lonely makeshift bed, in the dusty barn—when that soft touch seizes him, only to wax rough and violent, Gunnar falls to his elbows and knees, lifts his buttocks, pries his blond-fuzzed cheeks apart, and begs to be taken. That great weight sighing atop him, the soft brush of body hair against his back, the thorny ropes binding his wrists and torso, his attempts at grateful speech muffled by that heavy hand, that thick column of flesh stretching his nether-gate and stoking the embers of bliss inside him: oh, Gunnar has never been so hungry or so happy. The mornings after, he tries to veil his half-addled, thankful smiles; he does his best to hide how newly thorn-pierced his pale skin is, how his old limp returns after his master's brutal use of him.

NOW COMES THE NIGHT OF Yule, when the great wheel of the year pauses like a long-held breath only to begin its slow turn again, ushering back the lengthening light. Gunnar's father has snow-tromped down the lane to share a feast with the nearest neighbors. Gunnar has refused to go, despite his father's insistence that Yule might be a night propitious for courting Astrid, or her sister, Ingrid. Instead, he whittles by his private fire, waiting, praying. "Allfather, send my Lord to me," he whispers, sipping ale and watching the flames dwindle.

A little drunk, he strips, despite the cold gripping his little cabin, and climbs into bed, huddling beneath the furs. He's nearly asleep when that smoky scent fills the room. Trembling, he throws off the covers. Trembling, he positions himself on elbows and knees on the mussed bedclothes. "Please, God," he prays. "Possess me, Lord." Lowering his head, he waits.

A hand runs over his arse-cheeks, plucks at the furry nest between, and fingers his hole. There's a deep sigh, then the pain begins, the punishment Gunnar's come to expect and yearn for. Across his plump buttocks and bare back fall first the sharp slaps of his master's stinging palm, then bundled birch twigs brought down again and again. Swaying, Gunnar gnashes his teeth and tenses beneath the blows. When he was a seafaring raider, he and his shipmates prided themselves on their courage and fortitude. They told tales of Helgi, the legendary chieftain in the Eddas, so valiant he laughed as enemies cut his heart from his breast. Surrendering to his Lord's scourge is only another sort of endurance, one that makes Gunnar swell with devotion and pride even as he yelps and chokes back sobs.

"Red fire-glow on snow," murmurs his master, ceasing the punishment only to climb onto the bed. He fondles Gunnar's burning buttocks and oils up Gunnar's hole. "Beautiful serf. What service you will give me in the final fires." The blunt tip prods Gunnar's opening; the head's shoved in; the flare of pain shape-shifts almost instantly into flaming delight. Gunnar grunts, moans, and backs up, inch by inch impaling himself. The master chortles, grips Gunnar's lean hips, and begins a rhythmic fucking.

In snowy after-days, chained in the cave, guarded by the wolf, Gunnar will have long nights alone, huddled in his master's bed by the unfed but constant fire, to wonder. How could a god not know of that suspicious approach: Gunnar's father, returned early from the Yule feast, creeping across the garth, drawn by the sounds of his son's lusty moans? Surely his master allowed it all to happen, so as to possess Gunnar inescapably and entirely.

Gunnar is on his back now, eyes closed, grinning drunkenly, sunk in luxurious surrender. Invisible thorn-bonds stretch his arms tautly above him. He's bent double, his legs hooked over his Lord's shoulders. His master's dripping sweat burns his chest; his master's cock is buried deep inside him, battering his raw hole. "Yes, Lord! Yes, God! Yes, Lord! Yes, God!" rapt Gunnar grunts, matching the cadence of his captor's thrusts.

Then the cabin's door flies open, and Gunnar's eyes snap wide. Behind his Lord's hairy frame, there stands Gunnar's father, framed in the doorway, staring at them, mouth like a gasping salmon's.

The old man's holding a walking stick. He lifts it and brings it down across the shoulders of the huge man violating his son. With a pop, the Lord's slick member slides from Gunnar's well-plundered rump. The black-haired giant turns, smiling, and as he does, as if due to his sudden shift of focus, the invisible bonds about Gunnar's wrists evaporate. The blond warrior's up in an instant, heaving himself off the bed and into the space between his master and his father. "Sir—" he begins, but before he can continue, his father's slapped his face and brought the stick down on Gunnar's head.

The lad falls onto one knee, stunned. It's been long years since his father's dared to strike him, as he so often did when Gunnar was a child, before he reached his powerful prime. Gunnar's master lifts him, laying him gently onto the bed, and then his form begins to shimmer, shifting into a wavery green.

Watching in fear and wonderment, Gunnar can no longer deny who his master is. The cat, the magical chamber, the unseen bonds of thorn, the young Viking's warrior-pride reduced so easily to hungry submission, that need for bodily surrender lurking inside him all along made to flower so fervidly... Yes, he knows the name of the Master of Magic, and it both terrifies and delights him to be the slave and the lover of a god. Now, however, watching Lord Loki change, the terror grows entirely paramount.

Petite Astrid stands before Gunnar's speechless father. She sidles up to him, gives his groin a squeeze, and giggles. "Oh, Ivar Egilsson, I can feel your love!" The old man jolts back, and the girl disappears with a flounce. In her place, in rapid succession, are a burning bramble bush, a monstrous viper, an old woman with great breasts and wide hips, and finally a towering bear, its head brushing the ceiling. It lifts a taloned paw, bellows and swipes, tearing a bloody wound across the old man's face, knocking him across the room.

Gunnar leaps from the bed. From the corner he seizes his sword and whips it from its sheath with a musical, metallic ring. "No, Lord! Please!" he shouts, positioning himself between his downed father and the bear. The great animal moves forward, bending its head, so that its slavering maw and hot breath are mere inches from Gunnar's face. Then the room goes dark, filling with laughter. The candle ignites by Gunnar's bed, and there is his master again, in human form, looming over him. The Lord seizes the sword in his left hand. It flames blue and shatters. His right hand, clenched into a fist, he swings against Gunnar's head, and the Norseman knows no more.

THE SHUSHING OF SKIS? GUNNAR lifts his head. White is all about him, midwinter's heaped snows. The limbs of spruce flash by, caressing his bruised face.

He is naked, yet somehow warm. He is being carried, slung over his Lord's broad shoulder. When he tries to move, he finds his wrists knotted behind him with bramble-bonds as before, his torso, knees, and ankles tied as well. When he tries to mutter his Lord's name, he finds thorns twisted around his tongue, his mouth rusty with blood, hot drool oozing into his beard and freezing there in icy clots. He thinks of his father only once, the bear-mauled body on the cabin's floor, and then he forgets him forever.

"All is well, Gunnar, my golden serf, my snow-pure soldier." His master soothes him, stroking his bare arse. "Sleep."

The comfort and assurance that fill Gunnar are vast. He nods, heaves a deep sigh, and does as his Lord commands.

WHO KNOWS HOW MANY YEARS or eras pass? Gunnar cares not, sunk in timeless aching and mesmerized drowse as soon as Lord Loki leaves him. He wakes when the god returns, only to be swallowed up in compliant bliss and drunken yielding, wrapped in the embrace of a much greater strength. Barbed shackles and lengths of bramble-chain bind the young warrior's limbs to the bed, but that restraint feels not like slavery but love's purest promise.

By the fire, the black-bearded god feeds the blond-bearded boy mead and strong ale, sweet berries, rough brown bread smeared with honey, and the roasted flesh of wild boar, ox, and reindeer. He fucks Gunnar again and again: before the flames, bent over the bed, on his belly, on his side. In crueler moods, he rakes the chained warrior with his nails or beats his back and buttocks, drawing blood and lapping it up. In kinder moods, he makes of himself a multitude of men, and Gunnar finds himself splayed on the floor, quivering with joy, a mouth on his cock, a cock in his mouth, a cock in his arse, a cock in either hand. Sometimes Loki mocks the lad, coaxing him into vain resistance only to overpower him, ravishing him with the brutality with which

Gunnar's shipmates so often took the foreign women of Ireland, England, and the Orkneys. He spends his seed inside Gunnar's arse, inside Gunnar's seed-thirsty mouth.

After their lovemaking, Gunnar's master spends long hours with the shackled boy nestled in his arms, rocking him, stroking his hair and his wild, untrimmed beard. The Lord's fingers dissolve any creeping hint of gray, preserving the gold of Gunnar's youth. Before the Lord leaves, he tightens the chains, feeds the fire, lights candles about the subterranean chamber, and summons the great wolf. In Loki's absence, it guards the door, though to prevent Gunnar's escape or to ward off intruders, Gunnar neither knows nor cares. He has no life to return to. He has no world but this.

GUNNAR WAKES TO A DARKNESS broken only by low fire-flicker. His nether-gate is greased and sore from long ravishing; his wrists and ankles are thorn-raw; his well-chewed nipples ooze blood. Still, perfect warmth surrounds him, the happy glow that comes after flagons of strong drink. There is his naked Lord, cross-legged by the hearth, black hair falling over his face. With a knife, he is whittling a green stem into a point. White berries, like ice crystals or congealed sex-seed, lie discarded about him.

"Lord? Come back to bed. Force me again. Fill me."

"It did not promise, the spindly mistletoe," his Lord mutters. "The only thing in creation that did not promise." He turns toward Gunnar and smiles. He licks the point of the tiny spear, winces, and laughs. Placing the projectile on the hearth, he rises. As he approaches the bed, Gunnar, with shackled hands, cups the backs of his thighs, lifts his legs in the air, and grins with lascivious welcome.

GUNNAR LOSES COUNT. THERE'S NEITHER day nor night in the bewitched cave-chamber, so he measures the length of his Lord's absence by the times he wakes from sleep, numbers he marks with a stone-shard on the floor. Why does his Lord not return? The fire is growing low, and the wolf has disappeared. Gunnar's limbs shake with weakness in their chains; his belly rumbles with hunger. In his hair, nearly down to his waist, and in his beard, bushing over his chest, are streaks of gray. He huddles on his side beneath the heaped bed-furs, shivers, strokes his sex, and whines. His battle-scarred thigh recommences its throb; his Lord-welted back and buttocks heal, aching to be beaten red again.

GUNNAR WAKES WITH A START. The bed is shaking. The mountain is shaking. The earth is shaking. The hearth collapses into itself. Chunks of the ceiling detach and fall. The thorny chains securing Gunnar's limbs to the bed loosen, transform into loops of smoke, and dissolve. He rolls off the bed and crawls beneath it. The earthquake continues for long, terrifying minutes.

When it ceases, Gunnar creeps out. When he staggers to his feet, he finds the tunnel leading outside blocked with broken debris. The high windows, the candles, the tapestries, the arched ceiling have all vanished. It is only a cave, and the only light left radiates from the fire's last embers. The trapped, desperate Norseman calls out for his Lord, covers his face with his hands, and weeps.

HOARY-HEADED GUNNAR LICKS TRICKLES OF water from the rocky sides of the cave, then crawls through pitch black, over shattered fragments of ceiling, and into the fur-heaped bed. The fire is gone now; the cold is deepening. He's faced death so many times in his raiding parties, so often proven himself a hero. He does not dread death, but he wishes with a bitter wistfulness that his end might have been one more befitting a warrior, battling perhaps for his Lord. Weak with starvation and thirst, he rests his head on a pillow. He's about to slip into sleep from which he suspects he might not ever rise when a voice, a woman's, sounds in the chamber. A candle flares up and moves closer.

"Gunnar, Loki has sent me. He needs you. I am his wife, Sigyn."

AS THE SLAVE WAS SO often bound, so now is the master. Another mountainside cave. The dark-bearded god, naked, lies upon his back, chained down to the stone. Above him, the gray serpent yawns, its fanged mouth drooling blue-white venom. Sigyn catches the poison in a bowl. When it's full, she dashes to the cave-mouth and tosses the venom over the ledge and onto stones, where it hisses and steams, eroding the bare rock. Before she can dash back with the bowl, the seething snake-venom, briefly unobstructed, drips into Loki's eyes, causing him to thrash and scream and unseat the earth.

Gunnar knows it all now. How Loki gave the blind god Hod the mistletoe spear and directed his aim, killing Hod's white-gold brother Baldur, piercing his broad breast, sending him to Hel. How Thor caught Loki by the tail, as he tried in salmon form to elude the outraged gods. How they all bound him here, leaving him to suffer. Gunnar knows it, and so too do Loki's other slaves, beautiful men heaped by the myriads about the huge cave in their blocks of preserving glacier-ice.

Soon, Gunnar will join his brothers, to sleep till the twilight of the gods, when, after long years of unbroken winter, he will rise. He will fight with all the others here, on the great plain of Vigrith, helping Loki and his ship of the dead destroy the gods: Odin swallowed by the great wolf, Thor poisoned by the foul serpent, the flame giant Surt burning swordless Frey to a crisp cadaver and spreading the inferno of Ragnarök across the universe, till the seas boil, the forests explode, the mountains are ground into ash, and the charred heavens fall like a barn's burning beams.

Now, however, with icy water Gunnar, young and golden again, bathes Loki's face. He kisses his Lord's brow and strokes his chest, black fur sheened with the silvery sweat of agony and of rage. Loki smiles weakly, lips and sharp teeth blood-smeared. Green-gold eyes glowing, he growls Gunnar's name. While Sigyn holds the slowly filling bowl, Gunnar whispers love-words and promises, one hand resting on the bound god's hammering heart. Our blond warrior must swear his fealty before he goes to his rest, stiff and blue and naked, in a sarcophagus of northern ice. Sword at his side, fists clenched on his breast, he will sleep, dreaming of the day his Lord will melt that frosty slumber, grasp his hand, and lead him into the final battle, into spilt blood, sword-hacked flesh, and the cleansing fire.

1066 AD

I.

IN THE TWILIT ORCHARD, THORIR pauses. This spring has been unremittingly cold—Norwegian winter's stubborn lingering—yet the gnarled apple trees above the fjord are in full bloom. He reaches up, bends down a bough, and takes a deep breath, savoring the perfume. In mid-snuffle, he heaves a self-conscious guffaw, aware of how odd an observer might find the scene: a powerfully built Viking, with bushy red beard and shoulder-length hair, battle-axe at his side, sniffing delicate pink-white flowers. *Eirik and I, we are far more than we seem. May the gods keep our secret safe,* Thorir silently prays, rubbing the silver Thor's hammer amulet hung about his neck. He plucks a blossom-lined twig before moving on up the mountainside.

The path grows stony and steep, and loud with waterfalls, May snow-melt rushing off the peaks and into the fjord. It's windy up here, a velvety soughing in the branches of evergreens. By the time the Norse warrior reaches his blood brother's hunting hut, a humble structure set in a forested, resin-scented dell, the clouds have lowered, thickening into fog, and a light rain's begun. On the threshold, Thorir turns, eyes and ears wary. Were tonight's assignation to have witnesses, it would mean exile or death.

Satisfied that no one from the village has followed him, Thorir taps on the door, then pushes it open. Tall as he is, and so broad-shouldered, he must stoop and step in sideways to enter.

"Eirik?" says Thorir, shaking raindrops from his shaggy hair, unbuckling his axe, and shouldering off his cloak. The room's dark, smoke-scented, toasty with warmth, thanks to a blazing long fire. The straw cot's coverlets are turned back, Thorir notes with pleasant anticipation, and a goblet full of liquid glimmers on the rough-hewn table. His blood brother is nowhere to be seen.

"Off hunting," sighs Thorir. He places the flower-twig love token on the table and takes a tentative taste from the goblet. "Mead," he murmurs, licking his moustache before draining the cup. Weary from the climb, he shucks off his boots, trousers, and tunic, ready to slip into bed and wait for Eirik's return. But first he takes another log from the wood box. Kneeling naked on the hearth, he nudges it onto the fire, then with a poker stirs up the embers.

A footstep sounds behind him. "Brother?" says Thorir. Before he can rise, something cold and sharp is pressed against his neck.

"Get up, Norseman." The voice is low and hard with threat. "Slowly. Or I'll cut your throat."

Face flushed, blue eyes wide, Thorir stands.

"Hands behind you."

Thorir obeys. A sinewy arm slips around his biceps, pinning them together against his back.

"Who in Hel's name are you?" Thorir snarls.

"A sea raider from the Orkneys. My ship foundered in the fjord."

"What do you want here?" Thorir flexes his arms and clenches his fists. "We have no money."

"I'm seeking shelter, not gold. Looks like I've found it." Gently, the unseen intruder runs the blade's edge over Thorir's red-stubbled neck, then pats his throat with the chilly metal. "I believe I'll stay here a while, till my pursuers have dispersed. You're not going to struggle, are you? You may be brawny-built, but I'm the one with the weapon."

Thorir swallows hard. "I shan't resist you." Within the flaming forest of his beard, he flashes a grim smile. "But may Odin help you if we meet again. I can't be bested in a fair fight."

The man holding him chuckles, then nudges his rear with a knee. "Braggart. Keep your hands behind you. I'm going to bind and blindfold you. Keep very still, or I swear I'll slit your windpipe."

Overlapping Thorir's wrists, the intruder ties them together with rough cord. Thorir grunts with discomfort as his captor wraps more rope-loops around his furry torso, knotting them cruelly tight across his burly pectorals and cinching his biceps to his sides. Once the big Viking is tied to his captor's satisfaction, the man secures a rag over his eyes.

"You'll give me no trouble now, will you?" Fingers run through Thorir's unkempt hair. A palm pats, then squeezes, Thorir's bare arse. The burly Norseman trembles in response. Between his fuzzy thighs, his cock lengthens. A fingernail flicks the sex-head hard, inspiring in Thorir a pained jolt and a hoarse yelp.

"Goddamn you," Thorir swears, grinning.

"Damn me? The gods have blessed me tonight. You're my prisoner, are you not?" says the Orcadian, voice deep and rich with triumph. "You're caught, big man. I may do with you as I please."

Thorir grits his teeth, broad chest bulging against his bonds. His great arms tense, and then of a sudden he heaves a deep breath and sags with surrender.

"I'm caught. Yes. So it appears." Bowing his head, he licks dry lips, muttering, "So, sea raider, what do you intend to do with me?" His tone is defiant, almost amused.

"Ah, you'll see. I'm weary after today's travails," says the Orcadian, clutching Thorir's bushy beard and tugging him forward. "Let's to bed. Follow me, slave."

Thorir shuffles blindly, submitting to his captor's murmured direction. "Yes, a little to the right. Yes. Turn now. The cot's right beneath you. Down now. Easy, easy."

As soon as Thorir sits on the bed's edge, his captor slips more rope around the Norseman's ankles, fettering his feet together. "Wait here, Viking," he orders, patting Thorir's bewhiskered cheek. "Not that you have a choice."

Footsteps recede. Thorir hunches forward, twisting his wrists around in their bonds, gauging the cords' strength. *Damn it. Unyielding.* He listens: the sough of wind in spruce outside, the roof-pattering of rain, the thunk of the hut's door-bolt pushed to, the thump of wood added to the fire, and finally the rustling of clothes being stripped off.

His unseen captor sits on the bed's edge; the warm nakedness of a hairy thigh presses against his own. "Be easy, warrior. I shan't hurt you."

A strong arm embraces him; lips brush his cheek. Thorir trembles. With a low whimper, he leans against the Orcadian, then rests his head on his bare shoulder. They sit together for long minutes before the man abruptly shoves Thorir backward onto the bed, rolls him onto his side, then climbs in behind him.

"Here now," the sea raider says, arranging heavy blankets over them before pulling the bound warrior backward into his arms. For a while the two men lie in silence, the captor's fingers stroking the captive's long hair. Wind, harder now that the sun has set, whistles around the hut.

"You make a glorious prisoner," the raider says, pulling Thorir closer. The Norseman can feel the Orcadian's hard sex nudging his buttocks. A hand ranges over Thorir's fur-coated chest, fooling with the nipples, teasingly at first, then with increasing cruelty.

Groaning, Thorir twists beneath the fingers' insistent torture. When he tries to roll away, his captor only jerks him closer. "Keep still, or I'll fetch the knife," he growls. With one hand he combs Thorir's thick groin hair and strokes his unabashed erection, while with the other he continues to pinch and twist the bound man's tender nipples and knead his pectoral muscles with brutal enthusiasm.

"I own you, do I not?" The Orcadian's hard cock rubs against the cleft between Thorir's rump-cheeks.

"No. No, you don't."

"I do, my fire-bearded brother. I'm going to take you tonight."

The fingers abusing his torso shift now to his arse, probing Thorir's nether entrance. "I'm going to rape you, my well-trussed warrior. I'm going to ride you. On your side. On your belly. On your back. Deep within you, you will welcome my man-seed."

"No!" Thorir gives his head a frantic shake. "No, damn you, Orcadian. Don't!"

In response, the raider shoves Thorir over onto his belly and climbs on top of him.

"Yes. Oh, yes. I'm going to punish you for your depredations, for your savagery. I'm going to break you like a wild stallion of the moors."

"No!" Thorir bellows, thrashing and kicking beneath the sea raider's hard heft. "No! Let me loose!"

"Be silent," his captor commands.

"No! Get off me!"

"Be silent, I said."

"No, damn it!"

"Then I'll silence you myself. I came prepared for that." A strip of cloth is pressed against Thorir's lips. Snarling, he grits his teeth and shakes his head.

The raider grabs him by the hair and jerks his head back. "Open your damned mouth, man. Obey me, or I'll fetch my dagger."

Thorir musters another heave of resistance, then falls still and does as he's told. In a flash, the long cloth is pulled between his teeth and wrapped around his head one, two, three, four times, till his mouth's stuffed full.

"Now, damn you, behave." The Orcadian spits into his hand and rubs saliva over Thorir's clenched arse-gate. Thorir moans, tossing his head in protest, flinching as a thick finger eases into him.

"You need to be fucked, warrior," the Orcadian hisses in Thorir's ear, beginning a slow in-and-out rhythm. Soon a second moistened finger joins the first. "You must open for me, brother. Mighty as you are, now you're bound, blindfolded, and gagged. You're helpless. You're at my mercy." Fingers rake Thorir's right pectoral, fingernails trapping the hard nipple there and digging till Thorir winces and writhes.

"Your great strength is of no use," the sea raider gloats. "No one's nearby to rescue you. You have no choice but to submit to me. I'm right, am I not?"

Thorir nods. The pangs in his finger-stuffed hole are subsiding; welcome warmth builds there now, radiating through his groin, glowing in his balls. When a third finger's wedged into him, Thorir, shuddering, pushes his buttocks back onto the probing hand. When that hand's abruptly removed and his captor slips off the bed, the big Viking moans with disappointment.

"Liking that? Wanting more? Just as I thought. I brought something to ease your surrender," whispers the Orcadian, climbing back onto the cot. Something warm and viscous is rubbed over Thorir's arse-knot and pushed into it.

"Rapeseed oil. Just for you, brother. Just for you." Pulling the bound Norseman onto his side, the man slips an arm beneath Thorir's head, then crooks it around his neck, tightening it about his windpipe before returning three greased fingers up the big man's hole and pumping steadily.

"And now, I think, you're ready for something heftier than fingers, are you not? You're ready to have this sea raider's sex shoved inside you."

Thorir shakes his head, a gesture of protest that neither man believes.

"Liar." The Orcadian presses the blunt head of his cock against Thorir's well-oiled entrance and tightens his arm across Thorir's throat. Very gently, he pushes until just the head's half-inside. Thorir groans with hurt, teeth gnashing the mouth-stuffing gag.

"Back up onto my prick. Spear yourself. Or else."

Thorir trembles and grunts. He cocks a knee and spreads his thighs as far apart as his bound ankles will allow, then pushes backward onto his captor's oil-slick rod. Pain surges through him—the man's cock is considerably thicker than his bunched fingers. When the hurt causes Thorir to pause, his captor's arm tightens, cutting off his breath.

"All the way, Viking. All the way. I'll give you back your breath once I'm all the way inside."

Thorir gasps into his gag, twists his torso in their bonds, and mumbles for mercy. His pleas are barely a whisper; his head is swimming.

"You're not getting loose, man. Surrender now." The arm's pressure increases again. "Or I'll throttle you."

Thorir tenses and wheezes, then, with a backward bucking of his hips, impales himself completely. The pain is so great, his rear passage stretched so by his captor's thick sex, that tears spring to his eyes. *Thank Odin for the blindfold, so he cannot see me weep!*

"Easy, brother. Easy. Oh yes! What bliss. Sweet as mead, your body clasping mine!"

The Orcadian loosens his hold about Thorir's throat, allowing the desperate warrior to suck in draughts of air. He strokes his captive's beard, fingers his cloth-crammed mouth, pinches a nipple, and begins a slow, deep thrusting. "Open, brother, open for me," he sighs, kissing Thorir's fur-dusted shoulders. "Open yourself completely, and the hurt you now feel will fade. You believe me, do you not?"

Nodding, Thorir chokes back a sob and tries to loosen his nether-gate.

As promised, the anguish of the thick member sliding in and out of Thorir's arsehole slowly turns into burning bliss. Soon the two men are rocking together, grunting with mutual pleasure.

"Close. Too close," growls the raider, reducing his rhythm, then pulling out. "A break now. I want this to last."

They lie side by side, panting, listening to resounding wind, rain slashing the hut's sides. The Orcadian cuts Thorir's feet free, pushes him onto his belly atop a heap of blankets, and props his hair-coated rear in the air. He plasters Thorir's buttocks and muscle-corded back with ardent kisses, then takes him from behind. Rhythmically, the captor's groin thumps against the captive's broad butt as Thorir shouts and nods with palpable delight. The Orcadian's strong arms encircle his torso, rough fingers tormenting his tender nipples yet again.

"Now to finish," says the Orcadian, pulling out suddenly, only to flip Thorir onto his back. After hoisting his prisoner's legs over his shoulders and applying more oil, the raider slams his sex deep into Thorir's arse, bends him double, and commences a savage plowing.

Thorir rocks and squirms beneath the man ravishing him. His

bound wrists, trapped beneath his weight, have begun to ache, and the coarse rope's cutting into his chest mounds and biceps, but those discomforts are insignificant. To be so mastered, so roughly used, to be filled so full by the raider's great cock: these are pleasures Thorir knows only too well are penalized and forbidden in Norse society, yet he finds himself sunk in a submissive ecstasy greater than any he's ever known.

"Fuck me," he shouts into his gag. "Fuck me, brother! Cleave me like cordwood! Cleave me like the sea! Let me see you, brother. Please let me see you, brother!"

So thoroughly muffled with cloth, his words are unintelligible, little more than bass animal noises, but somehow his ravisher seems to understand, for in between thrusts, he rips off the rag covering Thorir's eyes.

He's like sunrise over sea. By the gods, Eirik, fuck me harder.

For a second time tonight, Thorir's eyes grow wet, gazing up at his blood brother as Eirik's pounding grows deeper and faster. How the captured Viking adores that cascade of blond hair, the braided golden beard, the sharp cheekbones and high forehead, the sea-blue eyes grown glassy with rapture. *And that beautiful smile, red lips that have covered me with kisses, white teeth that have bruised me and teased me, tongue that has showered me with bliss.* And that body, so splendid in the firelight—not as powerful or as tall as Thorir's, but just as finely shaped by seafaring, farm work, and warfare. That broad chest, coated with hair as golden as his beard's, sporting a silver Thor's hammer necklace identical to Thorir's own. Those strength-thick shoulders and arms, the orchard-blossom-white skin. The furry thighs, tensing now with imminent release.

Eirik spits on Thorir's cock and strokes it. He bites Thorir's chest, kisses his cheeks, his chin, his cloth-muted mouth. Thorir's arse meets his lover's thrusts; he slips his calves off Eirik's shoulders and wraps them around Eirik's waist, urging him deeper.

Eirik's face distorts. "Uh! Uh, now. Uhhh!" His pace increases, slamming into Thorir, jacking Thorir's cock, intermittently bending to tongue-lap the cockhead. Thorir shakes, stiffens, and bellows. His cock shoots thick white juice, richness Eirik captures in his mouth, in his beard. A few seconds later, Eirik spends, spurt after spurt flooding Thorir's fuck-raw arse.

Thorir's legs tighten around Eirik, holding him close, keeping his blood brother's cock within him until it's softened completely. Both men chuckle, then break down into hearty peals of laughter. Eirik climbs off Thorir, stretches out beside him, and tugs the blankets back over them. Thorir, arms aching with long constriction, curls up against Eirik, head propped on his shoulder. They lie there for a few minutes, pants subsiding, before Eirik frees his lover's hands and removes the long strip of cloth knotted in his mouth. They curl together, face to face, kissing gently, mussed beards nuzzling, while Eirik massages Thorir's rope-chafed wrists.

"Orcadian sea raider, eh?" Thorir says, nibbling Eirik's earlobe.

"I *am* from the Orkneys originally, as you well know."

"True. Well-acted, you stealthy brute. Just as rough as I'd hoped. You had my cock hard as soon as you held your knife to my throat."

"I noticed." Eirik sniggers.

"I loved the blindfold and gag as well. They made me feel that I truly was your captive. That cloth you used to silence me, it was a strip of sail, was it not?"

"Yes. How did you know?"

"Ah, I tasted the sea salt in it. Nice touch. How long have we been playing these tasty games, hearth-sharer, Eirik Man-Raper? These games of capture and surrender?"

"Ten rotations of the Year-Wheel." Eirik runs a palm over Thorir's beefy chest, brushing the fire-lit fur there like high wind caresses treetops. "You know that. Ten years of sailing the seas, raiding, and keeping our secret from the people." He fingers a white scar across his lover's belly, then one bisecting his breast, then one between his ribs.

"Any of these wounds could have carried you off," Eirik sighs. "How could I continue without you?"

"You'd endure. Till we met again in Valhalla. Let's not think of war and death and Odin's wolves tonight, or the battlefield's ravenous ravens, or the swan-winged Valkyries sweeping up fallen warriors and carrying them to their just rewards in the afterlife. Tonight, I want only to think of this life, brother. We'll be risking our necks in England soon enough."

"Yes. Next week." Eirik takes Thorir's hammer amulet between his thumb and forefinger and rubs it, as if evoking future luck. He's silent for a long moment, face averted. Then he lifts his head and grins. "We'll steal some livestock and burn a few villages. Those weak English. How shrill they'll scream."

"True." Thorir guffaws, kissing Eirik's brow. He grips his lover's arm, savoring the hard muscle there.

Grinning, Eirik flexes. "Not half as strong as you, big bear. You're as strapping as the Storm God. But not bad, eh?"

"Not bad? Damned godlike, I'd say. You're my snow-gleam, my sun-glow, my Baldur." Thorir kisses the small scar marking Eirik's inner forearm. "My blood brother, ever since that day so long ago when we raised the strip of turf, cut ourselves inside that makeshift earth-womb, mingled our bodies' lifeblood, and were reborn. Our bond can never be broken. We may be parted—by death in battle, or, may the gods forbid, ignominious illness or pathetic old age…" Thorir sighs, tugging regretfully at silver hairs glistening between his chest-mounds and encircling his navel. "We may be parted, but our bond will never be severed."

"Of that I have no doubt. You're only thirty, lover," Eirik assures him, patting the round density of Thorir's arse. "And I only a year younger. We have years and years yet."

"Yes. You're right. Yet sometimes my heart fails me when I think of how… Sometimes I wish we could simply leave here, leave our people. Become outlaws. Live together far from men, high in the mountains, where… where I could keep you safe."

"And what kind of Vikings would we be, fleeing from danger, from responsibility to home and family?" says Eirik, nibbling Thorir's right nipple. "You know they'd all call us soft effeminates, base nithings, if they knew of the lovemaking we share, and if we left our folk to fend for themselves, they'd be right. You and I, we were born to fight, to protect our kin."

"True. True." Nodding, Thorir musters a smile and shifts the subject. "Have you more mead, Eirik Man-Raper? Any food for your finely fucked prisoner? I'm famished after that brutal abuse."

BIRD CALL WAKES THORIR. IT'S barely daybreak, but a dove is calling outside, a plaintive cooing. He rises quietly, stirs up the embers, and adds logs. When he cracks the hut's door, all he can see is the dense white of mountain fog. Sitting on the cot's edge, he studies his snoring lover, heart swelling with ardor and thanks. *Lord Odin, Lord Thor, give us long lives full of fame.* Then, with a low laugh, he fetches from the floor the lengths of rope Eirik used to bind him the night before.

As sound a sleeper as Eirik is, Thorir has his wrists bound before him before he wakes. Laughing and cursing, the blond Viking begins to thrash and tries to rise.

"Fight me, Eirik Fairhair! You know I love it when you resist," growls Thorir, forcing Eirik back onto the cot. "And you know I always win."

"Yes, you do," Eirik pants, squirming. "Damn your strength. And you know how much I love it when you overpower me. Forgive me if I don't make it easy." He struggles even more fiercely, kneeing Thorir in the ribs. Thorir, in response, punches him in the chest, knocking the wind out of him, and captures his ankles in loops of rope. Eirik, gasping, kicks, but soon, despite his wild efforts, Thorir has his feet bound tightly together. Shoving him onto his side, he uses another length of rope to anchor the writhing man's wrists to his ankles. Inch by inch, he tightens the tether between his limbs, till Eirik is folded up into a ball, his fingers brushing his feet.

"Your turn, yes. Take your vengeance, my man. Give as hard as you got," Eirik manages to growl before Thorir gags him with several ells of rope threaded between his teeth and knotted behind his head. So trussed and silenced, he can only arch his back, whimper with eagerness, and wriggle his rear as Thorir climbs onto the cot behind him, strokes his hair, and tenderly fingers his arsehole, moistening it with rapeseed oil.

"By all the gods, I adore you, Eirik Haraldsson," whispers Thorir, positioning his great cock between his conquered lover's buttocks, ready to commence a slow, loving entry. "You are my life."

"WHY ARE YOU SO FREE of shame, brother?" Thorir asks. His face is glum; his eyes are blank.

Still naked, wrapped together in a great fur, the two warriors sit cross-legged by the hearth, sharing a breakfast of brown bread, cheese, dried meat, and ale.

Eirik groans, rolling his eyes with impatience. "Ten years, and you still ask this. I laid down that shame many years ago. Why are *you* so trammeled by it still?"

"You know why. Our people's code. What they would think of us. Vile, they would say. Unmanly. Unmanly! How I give my body over to you to be used like a woman's. How I savor it! How can it be? That I am the warrior I am, and yet I submit to—"

When Thorir starts to rise, Eirik seizes his forearm. "Don't leave again! You're always storming out of here, red-faced and ashamed after our fucking. I'm sick of it. The people are wrong! Can't you see that? Can you not feel that in your heart? I have no doubt that—"

"You have no doubt. I wish it were so easy for me. I can't understand how…"

Thorir trails off. Eirik scoots closer. "Come here, big bear."

Thorir obeys. They embrace. Eirik kisses his lover on the cheek while Thorir slumps against him.

"I understand, even if you don't. How many times have we had this conversation over the years? You worship the newer gods, the war gods, the Aesir, and their code of manliness. But my mother's a priestess of the older gods, the earth gods, the Vanir. She brought me up free of such limitations. *This* means that you are a man," says Eirik, squeezing Thorir's arm, running a finger along his limp penis, then softly pounding his breastbone. "Your strength, your sex, your brave and loving heart. You're the best man I've ever known, Thorir. When you take my cock inside you, when you put your cock inside me, we are still men."

"Sometimes I believe that. Sometimes I don't. Sometimes I think

I love it when you tie me and force me because..."

"Tied, you feel free of choice. Yes. And thus free of responsibility. But...to give up power and control to a man you love, is it not sweet? You do love me, do you not?"

"Yes! Of course I do! But we're warriors! We should fight *for* power and control, not relinquish it. We—"

"Thorir, am I not your blood brother?" Eirik takes Thorir's hand.

"Yes. Of course."

"For always?"

"For always."

"Do you not trust me? Have you not often said that you might be stronger but I am wiser?"

"Yes." Thorir smiles wearily.

"And when do our families expect us home from our hunting trip?"

"Tomorrow."

"Tomorrow, yes," says Eirik. "We have all day together, my bearded glory. Come back to bed. Please. Life is short for all, but even shorter for warriors. Next week we return to battle. Let us savor this time together, not waste it in argument and pointless regret."

Eirik rises. Pulling Thorir to his feet, he leads him to the bed. "I didn't finish, when you arse-fucked me this morning," Eirik says, stretching out upon the mattress and stroking his stiffening prick. "My balls are still lust-tight. I think you owe me a pleasuring. I think you need to suck my cock and gulp my seed."

II.

"Say it again, Olaf," warns Thorir, "and I'll do worse. I won't just punch you. I'll split your skull in twain."

Weapons drawn, Thorir and Eirik stand side by side, staring down their shipmates. Olaf slumps on the sun-drenched deck, rubbing his pummeled side. His jaw and right eye are already swelling.

"He meant nothing shameful, Thorir," pleads Egil as he helps his brother stand. "He was just joking. We all know you're the mightiest warrior on this longship. Right, Olaf?"

"Right," Olaf rasps between clenched teeth. "Just joking."

"Save your jokes. I won't be mocked." Thorir spits on the deck and lifts his axe Gut-Reaper in warning. "I won't have my manhood questioned. I've proven myself in battle again and again. And I'll make you fish-food if you speak such insinuations again."

"Thorir and I are blood brothers. We have been for a decade. Perhaps loyalty like ours is beyond you," Eirik adds, sheathing his sword. "As it is, I suggest you not anger Thorir again. He's always been hot-tempered, and he's bigger than any of you. We're only hours from the English coast. Let's save our swords for our foes, shall we?"

Nodding and muttering, their shipmates disperse toward the stern, leaving the two men on the prow. Silence stretches between them, broken only by wind in the sails and the splashing of the ship's keel as it parts gray water.

"You've got to calm down, brother," Eirik says in a low voice. "They know nothing, I assure you. No one would suspect men as powerful as we. But they might suspect, if you don't control yourself. Your rage is immoderate. It could make you look as if you have something to hide."

"You're right. You're always right, damn it. I'm sorry," says Thorir. "Let's fetch some ale and sharpen our weapons. I'm in the mood to slaughter a few Yorkshire carls. Remember those tales, what riches our forebears found on Lindisfarne? Who knows what treasures we might seize today?"

Eirik rubs his silver-hammer amulet and looks out over the glittering sea. "Ale it is, Thorir Man-Killer," he says. "And mead tonight, to celebrate the voyage home."

THE COASTAL VILLAGE IS SMALL, its inhabitants' resistance brief. Thorir brings down four men with his great axe; Eirik's long sword dispatches three more. Soon the ransacked church is billowing smoke, the streets are full of Yorkshiremen's bodies, and screaming women are hurrying their children toward whatever refuges they can find. In the churchyard, Eirik and Thorir, faces flushed with triumph, empty gold and jewelry from coffers carried from the church and bag it up while their companions torch houses, corral livestock, and raid food stores.

"Look here, Thorir," says Eirik, holding up an armband of red-gold. "Fit for a king. It will look fine clasped about your thick right arm."

"I found a silver brooch, good for your cloak, I think. Where did it go?" Thorir hunkers over the bag, searching through glitter, wind off the sea stinging his eyes.

There's a sudden sound, dull and sharp, like a drunken fist pounding a table, demanding more ale, or Thorir's axe embedding itself in a church door. When Thorir looks up, his lover is staring at him with surprised eyes. An arrow's sunk in Eirik's chest.

"B-brother?" rasps Eirik. He looks down at the arrow shaft, grips it, tugs it, and groans. A rapidly widening patch of dark red stains his tunic. He drops onto one knee, as if bowing in the face of fact. "Brother?" Eirik says again, in a tone of deep confusion.

"Eirik!" Thorir shouts, stumbling toward him. In the few seconds it takes Thorir to reach him, blood's begun to bubble on Eirik's lips and he's collapsed onto his side.

"Oh, God. Oh, Odin, no!" Thorir sweeps his blood brother into his arms; Eirik gasps with anguish. Eyes narrowed, Thorir pauses long enough to scan the churchyard for Eirik's attacker. *Hel take you, you fucking coward. Would that I could slice the blood eagle into your back, lift out your steaming lungs, and feed them to the shoats.* No one's in sight; anyone could be crouched behind the grave markers.

Muttering "Easy, my man. Hold onto me. I'm taking you to the ship," Thorir lopes toward the water as fast as he can, doing his best not to jolt his wounded lover. Olaf and Egil are just ahead, herding stolen livestock along the strand. "Archers! Beware!" Thorir warns as he bounds past them. "Eirik's been hit."

In a matter of minutes, Thorir's boarded the longship. With great care, he lowers Eirik onto the deck. "Get me blankets! And bandages! And water!" he commands the sailors within earshot. Hurriedly they obey.

"T-take it out, brother," Eirik gasps. White face glistening with sweat, he grips the shaft with shaking fingers. "Each breath is fire. Oh, Odin, it hurts. Please take it out."

"No, Eirik. I fear I'd rip you open. I'll cut off the shaft in a moment. Here," he says, lifting a cup of water. "Drink."

Eirik takes a great draught, lies back, and sighs. "Thank you, big bear." He closes his eyes and passes out.

GUIDED BY SPRING STARS, THE Viking longship shoots through the dark waters between England and Norway. Thorir sits cross-legged on the deck, Eirik's head resting in his lap. Stripped to the waist and swaddled in blankets, Eirik sleeps. His wound's been poulticed and bandaged, but to little avail, for it wells blood freely.

He's been insensible for hours. Wake, lover, wake! Sunk in deepening despair, Thorir strokes Eirik's hair and listens to his ragged breaths. Again and again, he presses his palm to Eirik's bare breast, feeling for his heartbeat. *Damn my helplessness! What use is strength if it cannot save the man I love most? Lord Odin, Thor, Freya and Frigga and Frey, you shining ones of glorious Asgard, heal him.* All along the ship, men bend over their oars, grim silence and hard faces bespeaking their sorrow for a warrior so admired and well-liked. Clearly ashamed of their past behavior, Egil and Olaf bring Thorir food and ale, muttering regrets and commiserations before returning to their posts.

The Northern constellations have reached their zenith and are moving toward morning when Eirik jolts awake. Blood gushes over his lips, staining his golden beard. "Brother? Thorir?" he gasps, voice full of panic.

"I'm here, hearth-sharer," says Thorir, wiping blood off Eirik's lips. "I'm right here. We're halfway home. Your mother's medicines will save you."

The two men stare into each other's eyes. "I don't think I have that much time, my friend. As it is, Mother would as soon scold me as save me."

"Scold? What do you mean?"

Eirik heaves a deep breath, back arching, handsome face distorting. "Oh, God. Oh." He seizes Thorir's hand and squeezes it till the wave of anguish subsides.

"Here, my brave one. Mead. For the journey home," says Thorir, keeping his voice as steady as possible. *All my life I have wanted to be steel or stone; now I am shattered glass. Without him, all the world will be ash.* Lifting Eirik's head, he helps him sip mead from the proffered goblet.

"Thanks. Oh, thanks," pants Eirik, sipping. "It's sweet as our shared nights," he murmurs before another spasm of agony knits up his countenance. "Thorir, you need to know something. Mother. She...she warned me. She had a vision sent from the goddess Freya. M-mother told me I might, that I might... perish if I took this voyage."

"Eirik!" Thorir's shoulders slump. Tears, long held back by Viking pride, begin coursing down his red-whiskered cheeks. "No. Oh no. Oh, Eirik," he moans, deep voice breaking. "Oh, Eirik. Damn you. *Damn* you. Why didn't you tell me? Why didn't you stay home?"

Eirik grins dazedly. "I was afraid you might think me a coward. And you know no one can sidestep his fate. Wyrd allots a man's death-day to him on the day of his birth. Don't weep, brother." Eirik lifts a wavering hand and strokes his lover's wet face. "Please don't weep. And don't forget. I will meet you there."

"Meet you? Where?"

"Where else, Bear-Might, Thorir Fire-beard? The mead hall of fallen warriors. Valhalla."

"No!" Thorir howls. Indifferent to witnesses, he cradles Eirik in his arms, covering his face with frantic kisses. "Don't leave," he pleads. Sorrow-stricken, he breaks down, giving in to wracked sobs.

"Wings. The swan wings. As promised. The spear-sisters. White-armed helmet-maidens." Eirik lifts Thorir's hand to his bloody lips and kisses it. "Remember. I will meet you there. I will hold you again."

Eirik drools fresh gouts of gore. Shuddering, he lies back in Thorir's encompassing arms, smiles up into his tear-stained eyes, and dies.

THORIR HAS WORKED AT THE runes all day, cutting his blood brother's name into the standing stone raised over Eirik's ashes. His kin and friends departed hours ago, leaving him alone on this remote ness above the sea. Free of witnesses, he's allowed himself the release of tear-bouts and enraged howling, but by nightfall he's drained, his eyes blank and dry. Done with carving, he wraps an arm around the stone, leans against it, and steadily swigs ale till he's flushed and numb. He pours the last of the drink over the grave, letting it seep into sod-pieced soil. Above, stars are beginning to twinkle over the headland. To the west, the sky's flushed crimson.

Head swimming, the big Viking sits heavily on the ground at the base of the stone, slouches against it, and watches the light dwindle. *Just beneath me. All that's left of him. All that's left of his noble face, his powerful frame.* For a few seconds, he's swamped with remembrance—how warm Eirik's body felt, how sweetly Eirik thrashed and moaned beneath him during their last lovemaking—then, heartsick, he forces the images from his mind, unable to endure the memory of lost bliss. He staggers to his feet, weaves over to the ness-edge, looks down at the sea smashing rock far below, and takes a deep breath.

Something croaks behind him. He whirls around, nearly losing his balance. A raven is perched on the gravestone; beside it stands a woman. Eirik's mother, Thorir is able to discern, despite the dim light and his profound intoxication. She's a tall, thin woman with gray-streaked blonde hair falling over her shoulders. She wears the garb of the Vanir priesthood.

"I know how much you lost," she says. "I know what you are eager to lose."

"Lady Astrid?" mutters Thorir. *God, she has Eirik's cheekbones. Two of her there. Too much ale.*

"He did not heed me. Will you heed me?"

"Lady, yes. Yes, I will." Thorir wipes his mouth and tries to stand up straight.

"What you seek you will attain in the king's service." The raven croaks again, as if affirming this statement. "In a coming time, a time of golden leaves, you and your great axe will hold the bridge. You will find my son there. I have seen him, a great dark eagle, lifting you into the stars."

She steps forward. Taking his hand, she presses something smooth and hard into his palm. He squints at it, brow furrowed. It's a polished black pebble.

"Rest now, boy. Then seek the king. He holds court at Trondheim. May Odin guard you." With that, she turns, strides off, and disappears into a soft mist rising from the sea. The raven croaks a third time, then sails off the standing stone, over the waves, and into the distance.

For a long moment, Thorir stands stunned, clutching the pebble, then pouches it. Lurching over to the standing stone, he slumps onto his knees and sprawls face down on the fresh grave. *The ale-moist grass, so soft, as if I were resting my head on Eirik's sweaty chest after we've made love.* He closes his eyes, listening to the boom of the surf, the whistle of the wind. He drowses, then falls into a deep sleep.

Thorir wakes to find the sea and sky pearl-gray with dawn. Head throbbing, mouth parched, he sits up, licking his lips. Unsteadily, he stands. Remembering Astrid's gift from the night before, he pulls it from his belt pouch. The black pebble's etched with a letter.

Wunjo. The rune of joy and fulfillment.

Thorir lifts his head and smiles, inhaling sea air and plucking grass from his beard. The snow-topped mountains to the east are edged with first sunlight. He runs his fingers along the name carved into the standing stone. Then, belly rumbling, he slips the pebble back into his pouch and staggers along the ness toward the village, eager for a hearty breakfast before beginning his journey to Trondheim.

MEAD-SWEET

THE ENGLISH POUR DOWN THE hill in clouds of hoof-raised dust. Hot September sun flashes on their helmets; their sharp spears and swords gleam like ice. They are a surprise, and most unwelcome. We thought them far south of here. We should not have come. We should never have left Norway. A journey needless and for naught. And we should never, never, despite the heat of the day, have left so many of our mail shirts on the ships.

My mail shirt I wear, however, and my sturdy helmet, for in a dream last night a troll-woman gave me warning, which I now see I was wise to heed. My axe Gut-Reaper is honed and ready, as am I, and so, as we Vikings retreat, hearing behind us the screams of slaughter, our first line of warriors falling beneath the English sword, I ask the king a favor. He knows me better than I would prefer. He knows, without Eirik, I have only my hollow life left to lose. And so he nods and passes on, leading our army's remainder over the narrow bridge, toward the east, where the ships wait, with our mail shirts and our reinforcements.

I stand upon the bridge. Today is the day I will die. So it occurs to me, but without regret. I rub the Thor's hammer amulet hung about my neck, murmur a strength-prayer to Sky-Father and Storm-Lord, pat the iron mesh that coats me, then in both hands heft my axe. The river flows below, a surge of gray, pearl-white where it tongues the stones. I must hold this place as long as I am able.

It will be a pleasure to kill them, the damned English, who brought down my brother-in-arms Eirik during a raid last spring, in a village we had plundered and burnt. I heard the deep, sharp sound, like the thump of axe-blade swung down into wood, turned in the midst of our flight, saw the arrow embedded in his chest. I carried Eirik to the ship. Stubborn, he lived halfway across the deep swan-road, the cold expanse of sea between England and Norway. I smoothed the golden hair from his brow, wiped away blood-gush from his blond beard. The men who once had mocked us, mocked how close we were, until our strength taught them better, taught them a respectful silence, they rowed, and they mourned as they rowed, they held their tongues and rowed under the guiding stars, while I cradled Eirik and Eirik smiled up at me, and I kissed him, there before the men, and I sobbed—most unmanly, true, though I hope my courage since has redeemed me from any charge of womanliness. In my arms, Eirik gasped his last. We brought him home, we piled his pyre, we raised a stone above him and etched his name in runes.

We will not lie together in earth's grave-grasp, as once we lay together, body upon body. He will lie there, on the ness-top above the fjord; I will lie here, in some rank English midden. Today is the only future. Today is the promise of eternal honor. Today is the day I own. And I do not intend to cry.

So, as my foes approach, here in this foreign land where my bones will bleach far from his, I think of Eirik, I remember how he and I made blood-brotherhood, our slashed forearms bound together, life-blood mingling; the way we made love in secret—in quiet caves and isolate moor-huts, dense woodland and scree-slope, misty mountaintops far from village or clan—taking turns as the man, as the woman, and how our shame diminished, if not disappeared, after a decade of

brotherhood, and we came to know manliness together, lying upon
and lying beneath, then lying afterwards side by side, sticky hands
stroking beards, hairy breasts, the scored crescents of battle scars. I
think of Eirik as the English form in lines of battle upon the river's
western bank, determined to dislodge me. I think of him as I grin,
gnash berserker teeth, swing my axe at the first lunging fool, bring
him down, spit on his twitching corpse, and swing again. I can see
their fear, and they do well to fear, for I am great in body, a head taller
than any of them, my beard like the lord Thor's, a bush of red fire, my
hair the same hot hue, hanging to my shoulders, those shoulders the
hard expanse Eirik so loved, my arms and torso like oaken boughs and
oaken trunk, swollen with strength, and I remember how Eirik loved
me to force him, to hold him down and take him, the violence we
spread in battle there too in the deep way we made love, half-hurtful
and half-tender, like two brute bears of the forest-firs, yes, I see him
grinning beside me, wiping blood from his braided yellow beard,
as the next English falls and then the next—my axe cleaves helmets
the way ship's prow cuts the star-spattered whale-road, their flimsy
English javelins bounce off my mail coat like trifling hail—and then
the next falls and the next, till there is a heap of them at my feet, and I
am shouting and laughing, drool dripping off my chin, sweat staining
my face, beckoning on the next man to die, and our army is, with
the gods' help, far from here now, and my name, my name, Thorir
Egilson, will be remembered as long as bards sing, or if not my name,
then at least my deed, and who knows how long this goes on, bless
the Valkyrie that brings me such a breeze, for sweat seeps down my
chest and back, and this is the fortieth, I think, and then from below,
a sharp stab, beneath my mail shirt, between my legs, from whence
came such a craven blade, my strength seeping fast, and I bring down
another five before, here, night-helmet slipping over my vision, and I
drop my axe, I lift my wet hand from my groin—it is a river, black,
unstoppable as any flood-flow, a mead-horn spilling irretrievables—
and I fall to my knees and remember Eirik's full lips framed by golden
hair and his great hairy breast and his great hairy sex dripping rapture
and his bones blackening within the pyre-fire and the deep-cut harbors

of home and the forests of mist and moss where we met and loved, and I fall onto my side, my great limbs like thistledown now, the scud of clouds, mere feathers now, useless, I am useless at last, and I pray to Odin, come to me, Father, lift me up, make me strong again, send me eagle or raven, lift me up, and now foe-shadows fall across me, what's left of the sky flashes with foe-swords, so I close my eyes and smile, for I know I will be remembered.

The voice that speaks my name is low and deep. It sounds like home. "Wake, Thorir," it says. In the sound is the faint beat of wings.

I open my eyes; I look out again upon the world. Below me, a rainbow's arc is fading, a rain-squall is passing. Above me perches an eagle. An eagle, all black. I lean against the ash-trunk and look up at it, its golden eyes, its hooked beak. Then I look down, and here is my great body yet, naked, moist with raindrops, though younger than I recall, for the scars I bore, the scars Eirik used to stroke, are gone.

I wipe wet from my eyes. Smoke is the cause; it stings my sight. "Look there, Thorir," says that familiar voice, and I do, peering down across a distant moor, where a pyre burns, and another, and another, a plain of fallen bodies. I bend forward, and I see the king, and many, so many comrades, lying on piles of flaming wood. Then upon a pyre I see myself, naked, a tangled mass of maimings, pale skin and blood-gash and even a glimpse of hacked bone, broken axe laid upon my chest. I wipe my eyes again, more unseemly tears, and then the wind shifts, sparks leap heavenward, and smoke covers my face, this living face here, that dead face there, and I close my eyes and cough.

The smoke is black feathers, teasing my brow and lips. I brush the soft touch away, but it returns, so I open my eyes again, and there he is, white teeth and red lips gleaming, eyes gray-blue, long-lashed, and laughing, as young as when we met, golden beard braided, golden hair bound back. He's clad in a cloak of black, cloak open to reveal the glistening nakedness I love so.

"Eirik?" I say, throat tight. Eirik is smiling as he brushes his cloak's edge against my face, playful as he used to be after lovemaking.

The cloak's woven of pyre-smoke, black feathers, eagle feathers, fire-flicker. Flicker and feather tickle my nostrils and lips.

"Eirik," I say again. I sneeze; I clear my throat. The smoke pours over his shoulders like storm-waves, like forest cascade. His torso is thickly hairy, as it was in life, a great muscled expanse, a silver Thor's hammer to match mine glittering in the blond fur curling upon his breast, the charm I gave him when our blood first mingled. His belly's lean, as are his hips. And there, between his burly, pelted thighs, is his man-sex, half-hard, which filled and fulfilled me, which gave me such bliss for so many years. I want to reach out and take his flesh in my hands, as I have hundreds of times in our past, but I am afraid, truly afraid, for the first time since he died. I am afraid he is not real, has not returned.

Pulling my gaze from his body, I stare into his blue eyes. He smiles, lifts his hand, tickles my nose yet again with his black fire-and-feather cloak. His aroma, oh so familiar, so long ached for after we were parted, washes over me—animal musk and seashore and the black earth in which forests root.

"Are you real?" I ask, pushing a strand of hair off my brow. I look down at my own form, as muscled as his, as young, coarse red fur coating me from neck to ankles, gilded in firelight. The stray silver with which age had dusted my chest and belly is nowhere to be found. "Are you real? Am I?"

"Yes," says Eirik. "Yes." He touches me now, very softly, fingertips brushing my chest. "Red-gold," he says. "The hue of Yule-fire, of dragon-hoard. Bloody and golden, my brother Thorir. Odin and I, we bid you welcome."

I seize him by the shoulders and slam my lips against his. His beard's soft; it smells of honey and beer. I grip him by his bound-back hair and shove my tongue into his mouth. He laughs, grips my arm till it hurts, bites my lip till I taste my own blood. "Hold onto me," he says, in between rough kisses, "and I will carry you farther." Then his arms fold over me, the black feathers and flame-points engulf me, and what's left of what's solid drops beneath my feet.

GOLDEN LEAVES FILL MY SIGHT. Gold's all I can see, awash in sunset wind. Eirik's muscle-hard arm rests upon my shoulder. I'm weak suddenly, my knees buckling. "Easy, brother, easy," Eirik murmurs, helping me sit in a pile of glittering leaves.

"Glasir. So is called the tree." He shoulders off the eagle-cloak; it drops into the leaves and disperses, a few dark puffs of smoke the wind carries off. Naked, he sits by me.

"Sick," I grunt, my head swimming, my limbs of a sudden feverish and shaking.

"Here, brother," says Eirik, arranging my bulk as if I weighed nothing. My head's in his lap now, the leaves drifting over my limp limbs.

"Why are you so strong?" I mutter. "In our last life, I could lift you into my arms with ease. Remember?"

"I remember," says Eirik. His palm rests on my forehead. His face hovers over me, blue-sky eyes and sun-gold beard, sun-gold hair, cascade of honey and wheat. "Here." He lifts my head and holds a drinking horn to my lips. I sip, and then I gulp. Ale—foaming, bitter, tinged with herbs. "Good," I sigh, licking my lips. Eirik shares long draughts with me. His fingers fondle the hair around my nipples, then the nipples themselves. When they harden, he gives each a fond pinch.

"I have missed you, big bear. Missed the musk of our bodies grappling together, missed the feel of your flesh inside me and my flesh inside you. When you're ready, Thorir, we will enter the hall. The All-Father has sent me to fetch you in. Drink now, drink more."

"More," I say. "Yes. You want my mind addled with drink so that you might vanquish me and bind me and take a turn atop me, eh? As you used to do. I know you, Eirik Fairhair, Eirik Man-Raper. I know your tricks. The wrestling hold, the blade held to my throat, the slipknot about my wrists, the grease rubbed between my nether-cheeks, and then the brutal taking." As I grumble the memory, my cock hardens despite myself.

Eirik laughs. "Sweet memories indeed. And more to come." He strokes my cockhead with a fingertip. Again he lifts the horn to my mouth. When I gaze into its amber depths, I find it as full as when we began our quaffing.

"This drink will clear your head, hero, not addle it. It will give you strength to rise. You must rise soon, for we must not be late for battle."

"Battle?" I take a last gulp, then, grimacing, roll onto my belly, hoist myself up on elbows, then knees. I gain my footing. "Never late," I say, swaying. "Lead on. Whatever's needed. The bridge? I thought I fell. Will you help me hold the bridge?"

"The bridge you held is gone, brother. You held it long. Oh, fear not, you were magnificent." Eirik chuckles. "But that time is no more. You fell, the king fell, the English triumphed, and then they themselves, mere days later, were swept away by other foemen, and the years passed, mead-halls collapsed, great stones crumbled, and Wyrd changed the world. You and I, we are out of time. We have passed on, over a new bridge, and now we move toward other battles."

Eirik rises. Glorious nakedness, he stands before me. Between my thighs my cock bobs at the blessed sight of him. Grinning, he takes my sex in his fist and leads me, stumbling after him, beneath the golden tree, through drifts of yellow leaves high and shifting as sea-dunes, and into the dark spruce forest beyond.

IT'S A MEAD-HALL, THE GREATEST I've ever seen, with a pitched roof of shields overlaid like golden shingles, with high-horned wooden gables that fade in and out of low cloud. "You know its name," Eirik says, dropping my cock and gripping my hand. He leads me around it. Inside the quiet of this woodland glade are wafts of other worlds: loud men laughing and singing, the shriek of sea-eagles, the break of surf on craggy ness, the sough of wind in pine boughs, the greedy crackle of fire, the tiny patter of rain on tarn, the distant spear-shake of thunderstorm. Here, high above the entrance, is a wolf carved into the gable-end, and there, on the far gable, a carven eagle.

"Valhalla," I whisper. "Is it true? I have made it then?"

"You have!" Eirik slaps my shoulder. "Think, Thorir! How you fought beside me all those years, how you held the bridge. What better sword-wielder is there? Who above you would Val-Father summon here?"

"And he sent you." I squeeze Eirik's hand.

"I come for those who fall. That is my reward. That, and time out of time with you."

"I have heard tell of women who…"

"Yes. Valkyries, my sisters, white-armed helmet-maidens. Swan-skins, not eagle-cloaks, but no less ruthless or war-like for all that, sweeping the battlefields like flake-dusted winds, choosing those who fall. So one came for me on that day."

"That day in the ship, yes." I take Eirik's head in my hands, run my fingers over his face, tug gently on his braided beard. "When I saw you die, blood bubbling around that damned Englishman's arrow, blood frothing on your lips… And you smiled as you left me."

"I did. Because I knew you would not forget me. Because I could hear her wings as she bent to fetch me home. Because I knew we would meet again. Here. Where fallen warriors dwell."

A fine mist is rising, droplets gleaming in Eirik's hair. Somewhere nearby, a river's torrent roars. Inside, a horn sounds, and the deep voices of men, and then the great door is thrown open, and out they stream, the great host of Odin's army. Scruffy and dirty, hairy and glorious, they are laughing, shouting curses and blessings, clad in bronzy helmets and byrnies, brandishing axes and cudgels, spears and swords.

I step back, gaping. "There must be hundreds," I gasp. They pass by, they pass by, they pass by. The earth shakes beneath their tramp.

"They are too many to count," Eirik says. "Every day further swells their ranks. We choose them and we find them, curled broken and panting in their earth-ends. As swan, eagle, hawk, or raven, we bend to them and lift them up. Strong men they all are, but to us they are so light, fragile as the new-born.

"Here, Brother Bear-Might, Wolf-Rage, Thorir Man-Killer." Eirik holds up a metal glint. It's my axe Gut-Reaper. And chain mail. And helmet. "Here where everything begins anew and warriors are rewarded, I have these gifts for you. And, if you are strong enough to take them, a bloody prize or two."

THE NOISE IS DEAFENING—THE clash of sword on shield, the smash of mace on helmet, the cries of the wounded, the trumpeting of horns, the cheering of the victorious. Eirik leads me over the plain, past snarling clots of men swinging weapons against one another. Through a stand of trees, a bank of fog, and suddenly we are on a narrow ness, a short spit of rock thrust out into wave-beat and wind-claw and the lowering drizzle. There, at the end, stands a man. He is young, pate-shaven, slight of build, weak of chin. His face is not familiar. He cowers, clutching shield and spear, wide-eyed, staring at us.

"He is yours." Eirik steps back. "Yours to kill as often as it pleases you. He will fall today; he will rise tomorrow, a fresh toy on which to whet your rage."

"But who is he?" I wipe rain from my brow, lick rain from my lips, striding further down the ness, axe-heft sweet in my grip. "I don't know him."

"He knows you. He is the English poltroon who slew you. On a barrel the carl floated beneath the bridge. With that very spear, through the bridge-slats he stabbed you beneath your mail shirt and opened your blood-flood. He boasted of your death for years after. Cowards often make up with cleverness what they lack in courage, do they not? Here on the plains of Asgard, at the end of earth-time, such cravens, for our pleasure, are lent us from Hel. They are condemned to spend their days as sword-food, axe-fodder, raven-feast, fallen beneath the hands of those who lived bravely, who died in valor."

The wind picks up now; the sea smashes against rocks, heaving up great gouts of white foam. "Here, hero," Eirik says, binding my long hair behind me with a leather thong. "Is it not needful and beautiful, to create the death of one we hate, one who has harmed us or ones we love? Vengeance is one of Valhalla's rewards."

I appraise the carl's bony form, thin arms, quivering hands. I lick my lips. "This is too easy." Grinning, I stride forward. "You, *boy*!"

He starts at my shout; he brandishes his spear. Behind him the sea heaves, splashing the land-spit with cold foam. "Stay back, Viking!" he yells, voice shaking like aspen leaves.

"We have time yet till tonight's feast," says Eirik behind me. "No rush. Savor your sport."

"I will, never fear." With a war-howl, I charge. The boy screams, a shrill, womanish sound. Again and again he feints with his spear, again and again he tries to dash past me, but I am nimbler now than I was before, so each attempt at escape I block with ease, my axe-edge hacking his shield. He falls to his knees beneath my blows, scuttles off, makes another run for it, is cut off once more. Soon I have cornered him at ness-end, in the lash of wave-spume and rain.

"Get back!" he pants, waxy face peering over his shield like a moon cresting a hill. The boy is so small, so weak, so terrified that I might almost pity him. Laughing, I move closer. Perhaps I will simply pummel him cross-eyed and leave him crumpled in his own piss, shit, and abject prayers. But then, as I raise my axe, with what last nerve he has he thrusts his spear. Aim more of luck than of skill, but true nonetheless. I snarl as the sharp iron sinks into my calf.

Bending, I seize the spear. Gritting my teeth, I pull out the flesh-lodged blade, jerk the haft from his grasp, snap it in half over my knee, kick the shield out of his hands. I grasp him by the throat, lift him into the air, squeeze his windpipe.

"So you boasted of my end, boy?"

Eyes bulging, tongue flailing, he's in no position to answer. I drop him onto his belly. Crabwise, he tries to crawl. I plant my foot on his back and raise my axe.

HIS BODY, NUDGED OVER THE edge, is wave-meal, shark-snack, fish-feast. His head I bring to join the others.

Eirik and I stand on a hill, among acres of pike-mounted heads. "Beside this one," says Eirik, gesturing. On the pike he points to is the head of an ugly man, with short hair like a dun skullcap, thin lips, hollow cheeks, and heavy bags, bruise-gray, under staring, angry eyes. I look into the bitter countenance and grimace.

"Who is that?" I say, juggling my severed English toy from hand to hand.

"The archer who shot me. Sometime soon, if it pleases you, you may slaughter him, while I enjoy carving the blood-eagle on the scrawny slave who slew you."

"Oh, yes!" I spit on his sour face, the man who stole my lover from me. Then I shove my killer's neck-stub onto the sharp end of the nearest pike. The eyes are clenched shut; the slack lips drool.

Beyond the forest, there are the blasts of horns and the excited whoop of men. "The feast begins," say Eirik. Taking my hand, he leads me down the hill of heads, around a mere, and into the shadows of the spruce. All about us, fallen warriors are grinning, gripping one another's hands, helping one other to his feet. I turn back once, to see a flock of black birds descending upon the hill of heads.

"Ravens," says Eirik with a faint smile. "They are very hungry. They start with the eyes."

ATTENDANTS—FAIR-EYED MAIDENS AND HARD-LIMBED boys—take our weapons to clean and polish, wash blood from wounds already half-healed, help us into clean tunics and trousers, and lead us into the crowded mead-hall. Spears rafter the roof; in huge hearths wood-fires leap. On the walls, mounted swords flicker with violet flame, casting light on the scene.

"He is there," Eirik says, pointing up the long rows of groaning boards to the head of the hall, where, on a throne atop a dais, a great-muscled man with a gray beard and a patch over one eye holds court. A raven perches on each shoulder; two wolves sit at his feet, occasionally treated to scraps of meat. The hoard-lord smiles over his clamoring, hungry men; he sits back, lifts a jeweled cup to his lips, bends to speak to a thick-armed, red-bewhiskered man at his side.

"The Gray-Eyed One. The Father of the Slain. And his son, the Thunderer. Thor is back from thrashing trolls in the east."

Maidens lead us to our places near the middle of the hall. "Our seats are good ones, thanks to your bravery on the bridge," Eirik says. "Nearer the All-Father than most." Side by side we sit, surrounded by burly-breasted and boisterous men who laugh and talk, swapping battle boasts and bawdy speech, displaying new but fast-fading scars, swilling cups and horns of drink.

"It is as the Eddas said," Eirik explains. "We *einherjar* fight all day; we rise from our new hurts and heal; at night we feast."

"All night?" I say, slipping my hand beneath the table to massage Eirik's sex. Inside my touch he is in mere seconds hard.

Eirik grins. I stroke his shaft. As a serving platter's passed, he stabs a fire-charred chunk of boar with his dagger, dropping it onto my plate. Next he fills my empty cup with beer, my empty horn with mead. "Not all night. Drink, eat, blood brother! You will need your strength for the evening I have in mind."

Harp music strikes up. I give Eirik's cock a last stroke, then with both hands we tear into boar meat and roast fowl, into great loaves of black bread, rounds of salty cheese, sweet bilberries and honey. For hours, we eat like starving men stranded on a skerry. For hours, we drink, hornfuls of the sweetest mead, huge mugs of hoppy ale. We laugh, lick foam from our moustaches, and pour ourselves more.

By the time the Sky-Father and his flame-bearded son retire, the hearth-fires are low, and men are staggering out, or wrapping themselves in blankets to snore on the floor. When I rise from my empty trencher, I grow dizzy. Eirik chuckles, wrapping an arm around me. "Sword-sharer, you are as yet unaccustomed to Valhalla's strong ale and mead. Lean on me." I obey, swaying as we pick our way through the drunken sleepers toward the great arch of the mead-hall door.

Outside, the glade is silent. Above us glint tiny shards of stars. "Come here, Thorir," says Eirik. With no effort at all, he lifts my warrior-bulk, one arm beneath my legs, one beneath my back. His eagle-cloak has returned, curling about us its smell of smoke and tickle of feather. Normally I would protest, a man of my age and might being cradled like a child, but instead, drunk and happy, I relax in his embrace. We rise, in a gust of wind, in a beating of wings. I want to lie back, close my eyes, and drowse, but Eirik says, "Look now," so I do.

Stars stream above us, and the seething curve of comets, and twilit clouds stained wound-red with last light. Below us flash night-moors, and the great expanse of glaciers, sighing their moonlit breath, and the flat black of lakes, moon-spangled and reed-edged, and dense forest after forest, and sparse hamlets, with their tiny gleams of candle- and hearth-light, and lace-flecked seashores, with their breaker-boom, and unbroken sheets of snow-fields and Arctic ice, where only gods can dwell.

Frigid air whistles in my ears. About me, Eirik's arms are warm. Now we descend, through scuds of cloud, into the farthest forest, into scents of pine needles and loam. Bump of feet on earth, and Eirik's eagle-flight becomes wolf-lope, the embrace about me shifts from feather to fur. Tree trunks flash by; banks of mist part.

Creak of a door. Eirik releases me, and I fall into softness. I roll over, face brushing the texture of woven wool. It is a low bed, in a low-ceilinged hut. Nearby, a small fire crackles. I give a groan of pleasure, and then hands are tugging off my moist trousers and tunic and Eirik's naked weight is upon me.

"Ha! I knew it!" I shout. We wrestle, long and fierce, but he is stronger than he was in life, and soon he has me on my belly on the bed, one arm wrenched behind my back, a knife at my throat. When I give him further fight, "Surrender, brother," he snarls, and the blade nicks me, drawing blood. Now I have the excuse I need to save face, to go limp and let him do what we both want.

"Always the dagger, damn you," I pant. "Yes, I surrender. Do it, Eirik Man-Raper. Do what you please."

Within a minute, Eirik has my hands bound behind me with rough rope. I flex, testing the cord; it does not give. Eirik is as good with knots in Asgard as he ever was in Midgard. I thrash around, rolling onto my back, trying to kick him. He sits on me to subdue me, stilling me long enough to trap my feet in circles of rope and bind my ankles.

Finished, he sits on the bed beside me, wiping sweat from his brow. I lie back, helpless, sex hard, heart hammering my breastbone. Wind's rising outside, soughing in spruce. A wet gust slaps the house. A hard rain begins its tattoo.

"Storm's coming," he says, rising. "You always did give me a damned good fight." He stokes up the fire; from a bedside table, he lifts a goblet and sips.

"Always, brother," I mutter between clenched teeth. "Always." Beneath me, I twist my hands in their bonds, straining till my wrists burn. Both of us are grinning now, eager for what is to come. The hard shaft of flesh between my thighs is nigh hurtful with blood-throb.

"Fighting you always made me feel mighty. Even when you won, even when you overcame me, through force or through trickery."

"Ah, you are mighty even bound. You are beautiful. Here, brother, struggle makes men thirst. Drink. This is heaven's hot mead—rich as man-milk, sweet as bard-song. Drink."

Eirik tips the horn; I take a gulp. My tongue sears, my brow burns. Forked fire flickers along my veins; the flames of my heart-hearth leap.

Gasping, I lie back. Sweat beads my temples, wets the cleft of my chest. Smiling, Eirik straddles me. His erection bumps my face, fat-headed pole rising from a wiry bush of gold.

"Gods, you are even larger than…" Staring, I lose my words in a hungry lapping of lips.

"In life? Another of Valhalla's gifts." He gulps more mead, then dips his cock in the goblet. "Will you suck me, brother?" The dripping head nudges my chin.

I am given no time to answer. With an impatient thrust of his hips, Eirik shoves his cock between my lips. He tastes of honey and smoke, sea-salt and bread. The shaft's stone-hard as the rock I raised above his ashes; the taut skin's soft as orchard petals, tender as cloudberries. From his slit I can already taste a briny drooling.

Groaning with gratitude, I work his cockhead with my lips and tongue, then slide my mouth farther down the shaft. Our gazes interlocked, Eirik fucks my face, slow and deep. He sighs, sips from the cup, strokes my hair, and impales my throat. I choke and chuckle, gurgle and slobber till my beard's wet. Setting down the cup, he rides me harder, both hands gripping my head, pounding my gullet, while I sputter and suck and fight for breath.

"Drink, brother," Eirik pants. His cock drives home, his crotch-hair tickling my nose, my throat crammed full with flesh. One last jerk of his hips, and his sap floods my mouth. Man-mead, gulp after gulp after gulp. I swallow, greedy as a bear in a thicket of berries, in a broken honey-hoard.

Eirik lies astride my face, softening slowly. Pulling out, he rests his cockhead on my lips. Happily, I lick off the oozy aftermath. The storm comes back to me now, battering the roof, the rain's softer sounds shifting to the click of sleet, and the crackling fire, eating resinous twigs.

"In Asgard, there are many kinds of feasts." Eirik slips into bed beside me, tugging blankets over us. He pulls me against him, my back pressed against his chest. With my roped hands, I brush his belly-hair. His fingers tug on the fur between my buttocks. "This hut is our home. Is it enough?"

"Yes," I sigh. "Oh, yes."

"Are you warm enough?"

"Yes, Eirik. I lost all warmth when you left my life, but now…"

"Do you want me to take you? To ride you as I once did?" His cock, sword-stiff, bumps my bound hands.

"God, brother," I groan, fondling him. "By Odin, yes. It has been…"

"Long months, yes. Long and bitter seasons."

"But how are you already hard?" I ask, amazed, squeezing his shaft. "How are you hard so soon after spending your seed in my mouth?"

"Yet another gift waiting for warriors here at the end of time." He spits in one hand. A moist finger brushes my arse-crack and circles my hole, probing gently. "Fucking as endless as the fighting and the feasting," Eirik whispers into my ear, his cock pressed against my buttocks. "The sword aches for the sheath; the sheath aches for the sword. Will you not open for me, lover? Will you not let me inside, where you are so tender, so hot and tight?"

I cannot bring myself to speak. Instead, I nod, nestling my eager rump against his loins. Flushing my face is the same shame I suffered on earth, most bitter in our first years together, those nights of wrestling when Eirik would win, forcing me down and binding me tight, when, freed by my own powerlessness, I would wax wild and forget warrior-pride and beg him to use me and would know myself, in the white-hot minutes of our coupling, as much a man in the being taken as in the taking, only to wake in morning's aftermath, burning with the same damned doubts, feeling both blessed by him and entirely unmanned.

Eirik laughs. "I know your thought." His fingertip teases my nether-gate, slips inside. "How desire battles against shame. That is what we Vikings were taught, were we not? That such a lust—to be taken from behind, to be ridden like a steed—was the abject and passive desire of a whore, and certainly nothing a warrior should feel."

Eirik pulls out, licks his forefinger, dips it into the bedside goblet. "Gods, your hole is mead-sweet." I tremble as his finger's length slides inside me, moistening me with heated honey as thick, sticky, and warm as blood.

"It was a secret…. what I wanted…I kept from all men…. save you," I manage to gasp as Eirik pulls out, only to replace one finger with two. "Had they known—"

"We would have been killed or driven into exile, yes. As effeminates and cowards, yes, as outlaws. Does not such shame seem—here, in Asgard's cold clarity—the stupid and misguided fear of a child, of a boy, not a man, a boy who does not know who he yet is, who cannot yet comprehend or come to terms with his own desires? I promise you, Thorir," Eirik says, adding a third finger, pumping my hole gently, opening my nether-gate further, "gods and *einherjar* know better. I also promise," he adds with a broad smile, "by night's end you will take your turn on top."

Roughly he rolls me onto my back. As he finger-fucks me harder and deeper, his beard rubs my face, his mouth finds mine. We feast on tongues and lips, probing and licking, chewing and wounding till both blood and spit tinge our mouths and stain our beards.

Four fingers are jammed inside me now. Eirik's mouth abruptly leaves mine, falling onto my chest. He finds a nipple, licking and biting as he did in life, hurtful and hungry as a wolf-whelp. I groan, I bleed and buck beneath him, straining against my bindings. Suckling, he holds me down with one burly forearm, then moves to the nipple's twin, growling low like a beast. I whimper and shake, arching my chest against his lips.

Suddenly his fingers leave my hole, and I'm thrown onto my side. I barely have time to catch my breath before Eirik's arm is locked around my neck from behind and his cockhead's nudging my wet arsehole.

"Oh, gods," I croak. I can barely breathe. Eirik's biceps-bulge digs into my windpipe.

"Ready, lover?" Eirik says, pushing his cockhead inside me. "Oh, I know you are." With a sharp, quick thrust, he's embedded to the hilt. I give a loud moan, not of pain, as I used to when he forced me, when he was overeager and took me too fast, but of pure pleasure. "Like that?" Eirik kneads my torso, fingernails digging into the hairy mounds of my chest. When I struggle, putting on the show of resistance we both so relish, he forces me onto my belly, his weight pressing me into the pallet. When I groan again, Eirik's hand claps over my mouth.

"Shuuusssshhh!" Eirik pulls my head back, kisses my cheek, and gives my hole a vicious cock-prod. "Behave now. You always were parlously loud." Pulling entirely out, he slams home again, then commences a violent arse-pounding, big hand gripping my face. I spread my thighs wider, as far as my bound ankles will allow, and with my hole-muscles clench his cock. He slams up into me; I slam back onto him.

"You like this, lover? You like this?" Eirik pants. "We can last as long as you like. This is Asgard. This is eternity."

I give a vigorous nod, and Eirik kisses my shoulder. Now the only sounds are Eirik's ecstatic sighs, my own hand-muffled whimpers and snorts, and Asgard's icy rain beating the roof of the hut.

FIRST HE IS EAGLE. I clutch one taloned foot, determined to hold on. His black wings batter my face; his hooked beak slashes my shoulder. About the room I stagger; he flaps and tugs, uttering sharp cries. It's like wrestling a thunderhead, enduring the claws of lightning.

I am surrounded by smoke. His form slithers from my grasp. Now the acrid cloud clears, and he is wolf, hackles high, snarling and snapping, darting around me. I lunge, seizing a back leg. We thrash about the hut. His fangs surge toward my throat; I shove my forearm between his teeth, pop him between the eyes with a fist, clutch his black-furred throat, force him to the floor.

Smoke fills the room again, and a sweaty, naked man is heaving and cursing beneath me, long golden hair in disarray, doing his best to writhe from my grip. I wrap one arm around his neck, another around his waist. We roll about, till he slips from my hold, tries to rise. I shove him backwards. He falls onto the bed, and I leap upon him. Seizing his wrists, I force his arms above him, trap his legs between mine, crush him beneath me.

We lie there, face to face, heaving breast to breast, straining and panting, my red hair mingling with his gold. "Yield!" I gasp, digging my elbows into his biceps.

Eirik licks his lips, wriggling his wrists within my sweaty grasp, his arms bulging with effort as he bucks beneath me. Then, suddenly, he gives a great guffaw. With that, his struggles cease.

"I promised you your turn, yes. Do what you will."

"Good man." I kiss him roughly. Then, with the cord with which he'd bound me, swiftly I tie his wrists above him and anchor them to the headboard. He sprawls on his back, unmoving, offering no resistance. Rising from the bed, I take a great draught of mead, then I study my flushed captive, his wide blue eyes, the tangled golden-blond hair, the honey-blond fur framing his smile and matting his chest and belly, and his cock, harder and larger than ever, jerking with the tide of his blood.

Sleet spatters the hut; the hearth spits sparks. "By Odin, you are so noble, so well formed, so strong," I whisper. Taking a mouthful of mead, I bend over him, cup his head in my hand, and kiss him, wine trickling from my tongue onto his.

Eirik chuckles, swallowing the mead. "What now, warrior? This, perhaps?" He rolls onto his belly and positions himself on his elbows and knees, presenting the hairy wonder of his arse.

"To worship a body for millennia, that is the greatest gift here. To know a beloved for all time. To exist inside him," Eirik mutters. Head down, he angles his buttocks higher and spreads his legs wider. "Give as I gave; take as I took." I climb onto the bed, kneeling between his legs. The thick hair between his buttocks gleams like sunrise streaking a wind-stirred sea. I run a hand over the hard-muscled plain of his back. He gives a little grunt as I nuzzle his crack with my chin, brushing his hole with my beard's coarse hairs. He gives a long groan as I lick his nether-gate, another groan as I tongue-dig deep. I grip his hips, wet his crack with heated honey-wine, rub my sex-head against him, and against his tight treasure gently push.

"Oh, gods," Eirik sighs, as he opens for me, as I slip inside.

"Tell me if I pain you, brother." I bend, kissing his shoulder. "I will wait till you are truly ready."

In answer, Eirik's flesh grips me from inside. And so I begin to thrust, but then Eirik begins to sob.

"What?" I say, slowing. "Brother, am I—?"

"No hurt," Eirik whispers. "These are the tears of the blessed, the fulfilled. Even here, outside of time, I have waited long. I have wanted this, wanted you. I have wanted you home."

Bending, I wrap my arms about his torso and press my cheek to his back.

"No more farewells," Eirik gasps. "Praise Odin."

My eyes are wet. I cannot speak. Hugging him, I ride him harder.

THE FIRE'S DWINDLED INTO EMBERS; the room is cold. Pale dawn glows in the hut's windows. Outside, in the evergreens, a dove is cooing.

I yawn and stretch. I pull Eirik closer.

"How many honeyed centuries have we been here?" I press my face into the musky-furred nest of his armpit, loosen the rope about his wrists.

"Fifteen, if you must know." Eirik rises to stir up the fire and fetch us food. I lie back, watching the sway of his long hair and limp cock, the way muscles move beneath the skin of his back and arse. Breakfast's more mead, sweet milk, cloudberries, honey-topped brown bread, a hunk of herby cheese. We eat side by side in bed. Beyond the window, all is white.

"The long snows have come. I must fetch more fallen warriors home," Eirik says, feeding me a chunk of bread.

I tweak his beard. "No farewells, you said. Shall I fight today then?"

"If you choose, hearth-sharer. You and I, here in Asgard we will part only long enough for ardor to flare higher, to sharpen itself like spear-head or axe-blade. Absence is only a whetstone."

"Are you not my greatest reward for a life of valor, Eirik? You, and the feasts of Valhalla?"

"Yes, that's true. Why?"

Taking the goblet of mead, I dribble a bit in Eirik's dense chest hair, smearing it over his nipples. We both watch as our cocks length, first Eirik's, then mine.

"Would the All-Father mind then, if, for my first full day in His kingdom, if perhaps…." I nibble a nipple. With a mead-wet finger, I anoint Eirik's cock. Bending, I take the head in my mouth, sucking tenderly.

He trembles and closes his eyes. "Yes, today, my swan-sisters might complete what's necessary. If that is your wish, hero."

"It is," I mumble, mouth half full of him. "Tomorrow," I say, giving his sex a last lap before rising on one elbow, "I will gladly swing swords with the best of Valhalla's warriors. And I will slay with infinite pleasure the homely carl whose arrow brought you down. I will make the blood-eagle; I will lift out his lungs. Today, though, what I want is not the delight of carnage but more mead-sweet fucking."

I straddle Eirik's waist, rubbing his groin with my arse. Moistening my hair-hole with mead, I spread my rear cheeks. Silent, we gaze into each other's eyes. Slowly, my nether-gate opens; slowly, I slide onto him. I grip his wrists, spread his arms, hold him down. Bending, my long hair tenting his face, I brush his beard with mine. We rock together, one man inside the other, as the thick snows of heaven heap Asgard's forests and moors, falling upon the sea's gray waves and the mountains' sharp spines. Wind beats the hut, whistles through the eaves, sighs through the spruce.

"They are coming. Together we shall share them—the final snows, the final fires, the final battle," my lover whispers, thrusting softly. Black smoke's rising from him again, swirl of eagle feathers and thundercloud. About us the hut's walls smolder and burst into flame. The roof is gone, and then the charring timbers, sucked up into a great whirlwind. I look up into rushing clouds, violet and gray, and shifting sheets of snow, and the emerald shimmer of the Northern lights. I look down at Eirik, and suddenly, in this fire-heart and wind-heart, I am again afraid. He smiles up at me, his cock driving deep into me like a blazing brand. The honey-gold hair across his breast begins to spark, then catches fire.

"Hold on, brother," he says, yellow flame framing his face. "Be not afraid. I give you my word: we are safe, we are god-fuel, we are past all goodbyes. Soon come a new Wind-Home, a new morning, with new gods and new sun and new green rising from the sea."

Snowflakes sting my forehead. About us the circle of fire, streaming red and white, rises into a roar. Soon my own body will ignite, for I can feel his cock-heat funneling up my spine, feel my heart-hammer glow and my bones flicker like piney kindling. I grip Eirik's wrists harder, staring into his blue eyes. I bow down to kiss him, from his gold-bearded mouth drink in the bonfire of his breath.

THE SAGA OF
EINAR AND GISLI

Fault with another | let no man find
For what touches many a man;
Wise men oft | into witless fools
Are made by mighty love.

—"Hovamol" ("The Ballad of the High One"),
from *The Poetic Edda,*
translated by Henry Adams Bellows

1.

I'M WATCHING WAVES BREAK AGAINST the Icelandic coast and remembering those nights on the island of Freysholm when old Patrick interrupts my solitude. He's panting by the time he reaches the top of the slope.

"Einar," Patrick gasps, face flushed. "Your brother. He wants…"

I pat the flat rock. "Sit. Catch your breath. What Thorstein wants can't be that important."

The Irish bondsman obeys. For a good minute, we sit side by side in silence, looking out over sun-streaked water and the crash of surf below. The morning wind is strong upon such a promontory. Along the cliff edges, sea birds nestle in black and white colonies. The sad call of the *tjaldur* bird, reminding me as it does of that time on Freysholm, only adds to my melancholy.

"Why do you spend so much time in remote places, Einar? You should be back at the farm with your family," Patrick wheezes.

"My brother's family, you mean."

"Your family too. The years overseas have changed you. You used to be such a happy boy, but now your black moods match your bushy beard."

"What do you expect, Patrick?" I say with a sigh. "Mother died. That's the only reason I returned home. I miss her. I'm grieving."

"We're all grieving Maeve, my boy. But you seem more than sad. What I sense is longing as well as sorrow. You've never really told me why you left Iceland so abruptly. What happened to you overseas? Did you fall in love?"

I try to keep my face free of expression. Damn it, he's too perceptive. He knows me too well.

"Love? I was too busy being a Byzantine mercenary, fighting for glorious Miklagard."

"Whatever you say. But I recognize the symptoms of lovesickness, my boy. You can tell me. Talk might ease your mind."

Talk? Not this time. One fact haunts me, and I must keep it from everyone. Even Patrick wouldn't understand. From what I can tell, Christians would be just as contemptuous as Vikings if I confessed this particular truth.

"Presumptuous slave," I joke, standing. "What liberties you take." Grabbing his hand, I help the old man to his feet. "You treat me as if I were your nephew. Is it because Mother was Irish too?"

"It is," Patrick replies, smiling. "I am too familiar, true. But I helped raise you, did I not? Where would you be without my counsel? Or the god-sent visions of your Aunt Aud? Did not our strategies help you and your Uncle Svein avenge your father's death? Now that murderer, Bork Ogmundsson, is worm-food, and his brothers and cousins outlawed to boot."

"True enough. Without you and Aud, I'd probably be dead. Or living in the wilderness, subsisting on wild bird eggs."

Patrick chuckles. "I can't see you living that way for long. A man with a frame as burly as yours needs lots of meat and ale. Well, young as you were, you were fearless, and now your foes are under the earth, and the blood feud is over. Now we have peace. And still you brood."

Peace? I've never known a day's or night's worth of peace since the agonizing events that followed that sojourn on Freysholm. "So what does Thorstein want?" I say, kicking a stone over the edge and watching it splash into the foam of surf far below.

Patrick's face darkens. "The *godi*, the chieftain, your uncle Svein, will be coming by this afternoon to see your brother about the upcoming assembly. Word is Svein also wants to talk to you. He has a business deal of some kind to discuss."

"Business? That's good news. I could do with a distraction…and some money. I'm penniless. Perhaps he has trading in mind. Another sea voyage would be welcome."

Patrick scowls. "This is bloodier work than that, I fear. Svein's messenger mentioned something about full outlawry. I think your uncle is planning to hire you to track down and kill a man."

2.

HE MAY BE FORTY-FIVE, BUT Svein Ketilsson's frame is even bigger than mine. One of the reasons why he's a chieftain, no doubt. His red hair and beard are beginning to gray, but I still wouldn't want to go up against him in battle. He's completely ruthless, most definitely not a man to be crossed. Luckily, he's kin, my father's brother, so he's always held Thorstein and me in his favor.

After savoring the fine meal that Thorstein's pretty wife, Kolfinna, prepared, my brother—a younger, leaner, smaller version of myself—and I sit outside with our uncle, sharing ale in the long summer twilight. I half-listen to them talking about assembly concerns and wait for Svein to bring up the business Patrick had mentioned. Why the *godi* would choose me for such a murderous errand, I have no idea.

Svein at last turns to me. "So, nephew, welcome home. I'm sorry about your mother. She was a fine woman indeed. When did you return to Iceland? I didn't see you at her funeral."

"Only two weeks ago, sir. I'm sorry to say that rough seas prevented my attendance at her burial."

"And how long have you been gone?"

"For nine years. I spent many summers with a crew of Norwegian raiders—we collected a good bit of treasure in England—and then with a Danish merchant ship. Then I sailed to Miklagard and served as a mercenary, guarding the city."

"So I've heard. A prestigious position." Svein takes a long draught of ale. "You're a fine fighter. Honorable and dependable too. How strong you look. So far from that black-haired brat I taught to ride. You're twenty-five, am I correct?"

"Yes, sir, as of last August."

"No wife yet?"

How many times have I heard that question since I got home? I try to smile. "No, sir. Unlike Thorstein here, I'm not quite ready to settle down. I'm already wondering where I will sail next."

"The taste for wandering is in your blood, I see. Your father was the same at your age, ranging off to the Hebrides and Ireland…which is why you and your brother inherited your Irish mother's raven hair. Ah, well, a young man as strapping as you will have no problem finding a wife when the time comes. Meanwhile, how would you like to take a profitable journey and do our family a great favor too?"

"Money I could always use. I had to sell almost everything I own, even my helmet and byrnie, to afford the voyage home. Lingering around this farm and taking advantage of my brother's hospitality seems like a less than admirable way to live."

Thorstein snorts. "I've told you that Kolfinna and I want you to stay with us as long as you like. You've been a great help around the farm. You can lift twice as much as I."

"Still, I feel like a burden." I wave away his kind words. "There are many far countries and cities yet to see. Gardariki, Frankland, Finnmark."

"Finnmark? Why in Odin's name would you want to go there when you could share our long fire and ale?" Thorstein says. "You're addled with wanderlust, brother. Stay here. Help us with the haying and the harvest. You could take your pick of the local girls. Sigrid Ottarsdottir has pined after you for years. And her sister Thordis as well. Just the other day, she asked—"

Svein interrupts. "If you go to Finnmark, Einar, you must bring me back Saami furs. Till then, I have another quest in mind for you. One less exotic."

"You're thinking of Snorri, are you not, uncle?" Thorstein's face goes grim.

"Snorri? Your son? What about him?" I ask. "I haven't seen him in ages."

Svein takes a bulging bag from his belt pouch and rattles it. "This is a great deal of silver, enough to make both you and your brother comfortable for many years. It is yours if you will bring me the head of Gisli Bjornsson."

"What?" I gasp. For a split-second, I feel dizzy, as disoriented as I did the day we raided that Northumbrian monastery and a young monk managed to club me in the head before I ran him through. I close my eyes and rub my brow, disbelieving. All morning I've thought of Gisli and the time we shared on the island of Freysholm. Now I'm being offered money to slay him? It's an irony too bitter to believe. I must be going mad. This must be another in the long series of evil dreams I've suffered since Gisli's marriage to Dalla and my departure from Iceland.

"What?" I say again, staring at the smiling *godi*. "Gisli Bjornsson? Why? What...what has he done?"

Svein stops smiling. He rises, coughs, and spits into the grass. "You don't know? While you were gone, Gisli murdered Snorri. Had you not heard?" He glares at Thorstein.

Thorstein clears his throat and looks away. "We were afraid to tell him. He and Gisli—"

"They were good friends, yes, before Gisli's foul slander. Which is why I've come to you, Einar."

"But..." I take a swig of ale. "Gisli slew Snorri? But Snorri was..."

"Yes, Snorri was married to Gisli's sister, Steingerd. That coward Gisli cut Snorri's throat while my son lay abed. Gisli confessed to the crime but refused to explain his actions. He was too poor to pay *weregild* in compensation for Snorri's life, and he had no kin left from whom he might borrow the money, so he was sentenced to full outlawry. You know what that means, do you not?"

"Of course I do. It means that…that he's exiled to the wilderness. His property is confiscated. He has no rights, and it's forbidden for anyone to aid or shelter him."

"That's correct. After the judgment, Gisli fled into the lava fields and hasn't been seen since." Svein jangles the bag of coins again before slipping it into his pouch. "Outlawry is too good for Gisli Bjornsson. I want him dead. And I want you to do it."

"But why me?"

"Because, the last I heard, you have reason to hate him. Everyone knows about his slanderous poems about you and that vile scorn-pole he erected, that image of you being penetrated by a horse."

All those years abroad, and still Gisli's betrayal tears at me. I grit my teeth, trying to transform the hurt into rage, an emotion much easier to feel. "I had hoped that was forgotten."

Svein frowns. "It has not been forgotten. You should have slain him for that slight."

"Perhaps. As it was…"

Svein chuckles. "Yes, everyone remembers that savage brawl you indulged in before you departed Iceland. You left Gisli bloody and bruised, as he well deserved. Still, the two of you used to range the country together. If anyone can find him, you can."

"Perhaps. We traveled about the country one summer, taking odd jobs here and there. We explored many wild, remote places. He might have taken refuge at one such spot."

"Also, you are fierce in battle. I have heard glorious stories of your prowess during those raids on England, and I remember with what ease you cut down your father's killer when you were only sixteen. You, of all our kin, appear to be best with a sword. You're nearly twice Gisli's size and should have no problems defeating him."

"All true, Uncle Svein," Thorstein says. "Brother, Gisli betrayed your friendship. After his slander, you said that you wished him a foul end. Here's your chance. It's your duty. Not only did he insult your honor, now he's murdered a member of our family, a man with whom we've shared bread, ale, and hearth-warmth all our lives."

84 "That is true," I reluctantly admit. "Vengeance should be taken.

But Gisli's been outlawed. He's lost everything. Isn't that enough?"

Svein shakes his head. "Not enough. Not enough. Snorri's body was mutilated. He was castrated."

"By Odin," I gasp, disbelieving. I can't imagine the Gisli I knew doing such a thing. "That can't be."

Svein spits into the grass again. "It's true. I found the body myself."

"A monstrous act. Gisli should be torn apart. Think of the silver, Einar," Thorstein urges. "The gods know that this farmstead could use the money, especially after the last few poor harvests. My debts are many."

"I know, brother, I know. Let me think on it." Finishing my ale, I rise. My stomach is churning and my chest tight, as if a dark worm were burrowing into my heart. "Thank you for your confidence, uncle," I say, gripping Svein's hand. "I'll let you know my decision very soon."

3.

I CANNOT SLEEP. I RISE from beside the long fire where sighing and snoring members of Thorstein's household are sprawled. Wrapping myself in my cloak, I leave the longhouse. Outside, in the extended gray dusk that is Iceland's summer night, I walk, wrestling with my thoughts. Climbing up from high meadow to higher meadow, I find myself at the shieling, where the livestock graze all summer. In the empty hut, I find the dimmest corner. Nestled there, I close my eyes. I try to sleep, but instead I remember.

4.

FREYSHOLM, THAT SHEER-SIDED ISLAND IN the West Fjords, how stark it was, and isolated, so far from human habitation. A man could be free there, free from human demands and familial expectations.

Gisli and I were both sixteen that summer. Our first day on Freysholm, we set up camp in a little dell sheltered from the sea wind. After a supper of dried fish and fruit, we bathed in the island's steaming springs, then sprawled naked by the driftwood fire, enjoying the surprisingly balmy evening. He polished his sword, a beautiful weapon with a distinctive dragon motif upon the pommel, then improvised bawdy poems as he braided his blond beard. Thick golden hair fell over his shoulders; his blue eyes shone with merriment.

Smiling, I stretched out, listening to Gisli's verse and admiring his nakedness. He was a good head shorter than I, with absurdly wide shoulders, a strong chest, and thick thighs. How pale he was, his breast and belly sprinkled with honey-blond fur, his sex nesting in hair of the same hue. I'd been attracted to other boys before—a secret I had the sense to keep to myself—but ever since I'd met Gisli at the local *thing* a year earlier, his handsome face and compact form had fascinated me and filled my dreams. What I felt for him was, I think, how most men feel for beautiful women. It began as sharp lust that soon intermingled painfully with a deep, tender, and protective love, a passion I've never felt for anyone since.

"Did you like that one?" Gisli asked, lounging in the long grass. Above us, a few stars emerged in midsummer's twilight.

"What? The poem? Certainly," I bluffed. Half the time I was too busy studying the boy's body to pay attention to his words. "It was fine music, little man."

"Of course it was. I come from a long line of skalds. My grandfather was said to possess words so powerful that he cursed a chieftain and seduced a priestess. What part did you like best?" Gisli rose on one elbow and flashed me an impish smile.

"Well, the part…that line…wasn't there something about a troll-woman and a fire-hall?"

"You weren't listening." Gisli thrust out his lower lip. "My poet's powers are entirely wasted on an oaf like you."

"True," I sighed. I was twice as strong, but he was witty and smart. Like my patron god, Thor, I strode through the world attempting to intimidate with my size, but Gisli danced through it like

Loki, sidestepping trouble, using his power with words to persuade people to trust and indulge him.

"No more verse then. Let's drink instead." From his pack of belongings, Gisli pulled a flask of mead, one of several given us by a farmer in return for a few weeks' work on his land.

We fell silent, both weary after the day's long walk and then the choppy hour we'd spent rowing over to Freysholm in a boat we'd stolen from a seaside homestead. The breeze grew cooler, so we moved closer to the fire. Lying side by side, we gazed up at the sky and passed the mead back and forth. In the meadows about us, the *tjaldar* birds called out their lonely song.

"It's beautiful here," I said. "I wish we could stay forever. I get so weary of the presence of men. Here, there are only gods."

"Gods, yes. Though they must tolerate the preshence of two men tonight." Gisli nudged my shoulder. His speech was already slurring. He'd never been able to hold his drink as well as I. "I hope the spirits here will forgive our intrusion. And speaking of things otherworldly and divine..."

He took the flask from me and drank. "To Freya, the goddess of love," he toasted. "And her brother Frey. May our cocks grow as large as his."

He took another slug, then, reaching down, gave his prick a tug. To my surprise, it was half-hard. The sight sent stiffness to my own sex. Flushing, I rolled onto my belly to hide my arousal.

Gisli's exposed body often had that effect on me. For a year, we'd been spending time together—traveling, working side by side, fishing, bathing and swimming, practicing our sword-play, sometimes sleeping in the same bed—and every time I'd seen him half-clothed or unclothed entirely, my cursed cock threatened to betray me. He must have noticed at some point, and I lived in fear that he might mention the unseemly fact to someone else.

Forcing a grin, I took the flask he offered. "You speak of the gods, yet you tug your prick. Blasphemy, is it not?"

"Not at all. The gods have a sense of humor. And Frey and Freya are the Lord and Lady of pleasure and fertility, right? I think, I think…" Gisli moved closer and whispered in my ear, pretending that an audience might be eavesdropping despite the remote nature of the place. "I think you should leave off raiding and farming and instead become Frey's priest."

Unnerved by his naked nearness, I pushed Gisli away and mustered a laugh. "Me? A priest? And why would you say that?"

Gisli snatched the mead back and downed the rest. "This flask's done, damn it. So it's back to verse, I fear." He sat cross-legged. I lay on my back and studied his finely shaped torso, the golden gleaming of his chest hair in the firelight, as he recited another impromptu poem.

> Einar, my berserker brother,
> with the furry face and body of a bear,
> his great dick-sword may be heavy,
> but he hefts it every day,
> aroused by all he sees:
> the she-goat's milky udders,
> the stallion's swinging bollocks,
> the wrinkled dugs of Ingrid's aunt.
> His quest is for myriad sheaths
> to raid, both cunt and arse.
> With his Viking ship's cock-prow
> he plows the virgin waves,
> shoots spume onto the skerries.
> His hot springs are ageless, eternal,
> and no one bears a blade as great as his.
> Should not such a massive weapon
> be offered to the god Frey?
> Should not my burly bear-brother
> become a priest of pricks?

"Glorious," I said, both pleased and unsettled. The poem was proof that he'd noticed both the size of my sex and its propensity to rise in his presence. "It's true that my prick's a treasure. As for you, little man, what a tiny member," I joked, trying to hide my unease. "At least the gods have compensated you with a golden tongue."

"Whore-son! Brain-maimed giant! My prick's more than adequate. At least that's what Ingrid says." To my amazement, he spat into his palm, moistened his dick, and played with the head of it. In seconds, he was fully hard. He wasn't as big as I down there, but his member was of impressive length, especially on a man of short stature.

"Ingrid? Right," I said, staring at him, watching his hand move. I knew I should look away, but I couldn't. Many was the time we'd shared a bed back home or sprawled near a fire in the wilderness, and during the last few weeks of our travels, I'd awakened nearly every morning to the welcome pleasure of Gisli nestling against me beneath our shared blanket, but he'd never made such a show of his prick before. "Ingrid, and Sigrid, and Astrid, and Dalla, and Thordis, and…Gudrun," I said, voice close to shaking.

"Oh, yes. I've had all of them. Or so it's said." Gisli giggled before adding more spit. He'd moved past fondling; he was slowly stroking himself. "Soon my brood will fill the district." He closed his eyes and sighed. "My seed will match the waters of Geysir. Ah, this feels good. Do I offend you, Einar? I'm being a bawdy fool, I suppose. Far too much mead."

"I'm…" I cleared my throat. "I'm not offended. If you feel the need to… I think…most men…"

"I think they do, yes," Gisli said. "My older brother Gunnar and I…once…the summer before he died in that battle on the ice…"

"Yes?" I wanted to roll on top of him and kiss him, but I resisted the impulse.

"Yes. A few times in our tent at the *thing*. Side by side. Like we are now. Do you, Einar? Pleasure yourself like this?" Gisli opened one eye and grinned at me.

"I….I do. Sometimes."

"Show me. Now it's feeling so good I can't stop, and I don't want to be the only man Frey makes a fool of tonight."

I couldn't believe what I was hearing. "You want me to…?"

"I want you to work your cock. Why not? We're alone here. Be brave, man. There are no cunts about. Just our hands."

"True." I rolled over onto my side, facing him, and gripped my very excited member. Our gazes interlocked. Part of me wanted to look away, to get up and leave, and part of me wanted to stay there forever, staring into his blue eyes as I stroked myself. How many times had I pleasured myself that way while thinking of him? And suddenly, thank the glorious gods of earth and sky, we were there together, naked, Gisli and I, our pricks in our hands. It was bliss I'd often imagined but never thought would come to pass.

"Feel good?" Gisli chuckled. With his free hand, he began caressing his chest, the tiny points of his nipples swathed in yellow hair. How often I'd longed to touch and taste him there.

"Y-yes. Yes."

Gisli scooted closer, till we were mere inches apart. "You should have been named Thorstein instead of your brother."

"And why is that?" I said, following his lead by adding spit to the blissful process.

"Because that's quite the hammer you have." Gisli dropped his dick and cupped my balls in his hand. The gasp I tried to suppress escaped me nonetheless. He nudged my hand aside and clutched my cock.

"Gisli…"

My friend didn't respond. Instead he began stroking my sex-shaft. Emboldened, I took his prick in my hand. His flesh was hot and hard, the sex-head moist with juice.

"Ah, yes, that's good," he sighed. He gave me a mischievous smile, his blue eyes glassy with drink. "Touch me, Einar. No one's about. Let's do what we please."

After a year of yearning for him, I needed no further permission. "By the gods, man, so we will." Gripping his long hair, I pulled his head back. I kissed him hard on the mouth. He kissed me back, pushing his tongue between my lips. For a long time, we were joined in passionate kissing and the tight gripping of one another's cocks.

"I've wanted this so badly, Einar," Gisli whispered.

"I as well!" I blurted. My long-suppressed adoration for him made the truth gush from me. "You are a glorious man, Gisli Bjornsson! Golden as the sun. Your body is a wonder, a gift from the gods. How I cherish you."

I rolled him onto his back and lay on top of him, kissing him fervently. I kneaded his muscles—his hard shoulders and arms, the furry mounds of his breast. I lapped at the tiny nipples there. His response was a groan of pleasure, and so I licked them harder. He clasped my head tightly, urging me on with both word and gesture.

"Yes. Yes, Einar. Harder. Yes."

I sucked his nipples, at the same time fisting his prick. He sighed and tensed beneath me. I made love to him like that, growing rougher and rougher, till he was wincing, his thighs were shaking, and both my beard and his chest hair were sodden with my spit.

"Shall I finish you?" I said, lifting my head from his broad breast. His cock pulsed and oozed in my palm.

"I don't want to spend yet. On your back, Einar," Gisli ordered. "Now I must taste you."

I did as he said. He lay on top of me, kissing the Thor's hammer that hung about my neck before moving his attentions to my chest. For a time, he pleasured me the same way I had him, sucking my nipples, biting my breast-flesh, pulling at the black hair upon my body with his teeth, and sliding his hand up and down my prick. Eventually, he slipped lower, brushing first my belly with his braided beard, then my groin. Then, to my shock and shuddering delight, he licked my cock and took me into his mouth.

The sensations of his warm tongue on me, the sliding of his tight lips up and down my shaft were a greater bliss than any I'd known. I lost all control, growling and thrashing, gripping him by the shoulders and thrusting into him. In no time at all, I'd spent into his mouth. He gulped my seed as eagerly as earlier he'd gulped the mead. A few seconds later, his own seed spattered my thigh.

5.

WE CURLED TOGETHER BENEATH A blanket by the fire. A crescent moon had risen. The sea's sound was constant, as was the wind's, soothing music bringing sleep. We drifted off, nestled in each other's arms.

Near sunrise, I woke, my sex hard again. Gisli's bare back was pressed against my chest. I wrapped an arm around him, ground my groin against his rear, and roused him with another bout of kisses. Feeling bolder than the night before, I fondled his beautiful arse. He didn't resist my fingers' attentions; indeed, he nestled even closer.

I kneaded his buttocks, then rolled him onto his side and took his cock into my mouth. His flesh was salty, musky. His sex-sap smeared my tongue. Gisli rode my face, sighing and shaking. I spit-moistened a finger, played with the hair in his arse-cleft, found his hole, and rubbed it. When I pushed my fingertip inside him, he tensed and moaned.

"Please, Gisli. Please? May I? Please? I've dreamed of…for months now, I've wanted…"

Gisli didn't reply. He gazed intently into my eyes. Doubt swept across his face for a moment, then he gave me a faint smile. He pushed me off him, only to roll over onto his belly and spread his thighs.

"Yes, Einar," he murmured. "Yes."

Hands shaking, I moistened us both with copious amounts of spit before lying upon him, wrapping an arm around his torso, and nudging my sex-head against his nether-gate. Eager as I was, I did my best to go slowly, afraid of hurting him, afraid he might change his mind.

"Easy, Einar. Easy," Gisli whimpered, quivering as I edged the tip of my cock inside him. I pulled out to add more spit, then eased into him again. He gasped and flinched as my cockhead pushed past the resistance of his arse-ring.

"Ah, by the gods," I groaned, thrusting into his hole's enveloping heat. "So tight. It's pure bliss."

"Einar, ah! It burns, man. Uhh!" Gisli's hands clawed grass, as if he were trying to escape. Releasing a pained moan, he began to struggle beneath me.

I should have pulled out, but the ecstasy of having my cock surrounded by the snug muscles of his arse-sheath was too profound. Instead, I pressed a hand over his mouth, held him down with my much greater strength, slid the rest of my prick into him, and began a gentle thrusting. Gisli moaned, writhed, and shook his head. My palm muffled his pleas.

"Shhhhhh," I muttered. Embedded inside him, I paused in my thrusts. "Be easy, Gisli. Let us lie still till your body grows accustomed to me. Open to me, battle-brother. Please. This rapture's god-sent. Please don't make me stop. Please. I'm begging you."

Beneath me, Gisli's struggles ceased. He panted against my hand. I soothed him, kissing his freckled shoulders and stroking his beard-braid, his whiskered cheeks. I rolled us onto our sides and caressed his nipples and groin. His cock was nearly limp, but after a minute of my ardor-eager attentions, it resumed its former thickness, growing sticky at the tip.

"May I continue?" I nibbled Gisli's ear and nuzzled his neck. I pulled halfway out, then ever so slowly pushed into him again.

Gisli nodded. I resumed my thrusts, moving in and out of him, growling with the sheer bliss of it. To my relief, his responses gradually shifted from pained endurance to building delight. Goaded on by his pleasure, I prick-prodded him deeper and deeper, faster and faster. Soon, he began groaning lustily against my hand, working his own prick and grinding his arse against my groin. We finished together as the rising sun burnished the sea.

6.

NEARLY A DECADE AGO. I roll over in the hay, close to tears, fondling my sex, pretending that the fist I hump is his rear. Too well I remember how it felt to be inside him. Too well I remember his arse, the perfect curves of it, the skin soft as spring petals and pale as the long winter's descent, the wiry copse of golden hair in his crevice, the tight pink entrance into paradise. Too well I remember how happily he groaned and sighed beneath me, the joy our bodies found together matching any gift reserved for the shining gods of Asgard.

Grunting, I finish in my hand, and instantly the self-brought pleasure rots into regret. Now I'm remembering what I'd rather not: what happened after those three rapturous days and mead-mad nights, nights in which he submitted to my cock and took my seed inside him again and again. Gisli turned away from me. Gisli betrayed me.

7.

My mother Maeve used to tell me Irish stories when I was a child. One of them involved a band of men who traveled to a faerie island in the west. They lingered there for years, savoring magical delights. But then they grew homesick and wished to see Ireland once more. The faeries let them depart, but first they warned them that, during the time they had spent in the Land of the Blessed, a hundred years had passed in the mortal world. Ireland would not be the same place they left, and if they were to touch the earth, the time they had sidestepped would catch up to them. And so it was. One of them strode onto the shore and immediately crumbled into dust.

I thought of that tale when dwindling provisions caused Gisli and me to leave Freysholm. Gisli's mood changed, like a man awakened from a dream or a drunk finally sober. I could guess why. In our Norse lands, the gravest insult is to accuse a man of sexual submission. I could almost see the unspoken shame flooding him. My cock had entered his arse, not once but several times. He had not been forced. Willingly he had given himself to me as a woman would a man, and the spending of his seed was sticky proof that such surrender gave him pleasure. What would people think of him if they knew? He would be thought weak, effeminate, unmanly. No one would respect him. He would be mocked. He might even be outlawed.

Gisli insisted that we truncate the further wandering we had planned and head home. All the way back, he refused to meet my eyes. When we reached our native district, we parted in awkward silence. For the rest of the summer, he avoided me at local assemblies. At the celebration of Winter Nights, he ignored me entirely, spending much of the time making a grand show of flirting with young women.

After a while, I was thankful for his aloofness, thankful that we rarely crossed paths. How his body haunted me. To be near him but unable to touch him was agony. Why had the gods given me such a gift only to wrest it away?

Lying alone in the lengthening autumn dark, remembering our naked summer nights together, aching to have him beside me, I had lots of time to think. Why was I so free of the shame that poisoned him? Partly because I had taken Gisli, he had not taken me. But I would have given myself to him that way if he'd asked. By definition, the delight two men take together is manly, not womanly.

Perhaps it was my mother's Celtic blood that saved me from shame. Her Irish goddess was said to approve of all forms of love and pleasure. The times I'd spent in Ireland as a boy, visiting kin with her, I'd heard bawdy stories of young men sleeping together on animal skins and giving their bodies to bedmates without guilt. The tone of such tales was not scorn but amusement.

On my father's side, my Aunt Aud had raised me to respect not only the Aesir—warlike Thor and Allfather Odin and their manly deeds—but the Vanir as well, the very gods Gisli had toasted on the island. Frey was the god of fertility, represented in his temples by a figure with a large, erect phallus, and Freya was the seductive goddess of love. The tales about them seemed to suggest that they celebrated anything that gave the body rapture.

In addition, my father was somewhat of a freethinker. He'd taught me that a man should live as he wants, make his own rules, and live as free of others' expectations as possible. "Yes, your reputation's of great importance," he used to say as we worked the fields, "but proper discretion and silence on certain subjects can allow you to attain both a respectable public image and a fulfilling private life. There is, after all, no reason for everyone to know everything. Keep to yourself. Choose solitude over poor company. Do what you feel is right, not what people say."

So I thanked the gods for my upbringing, pitied Gisli his guilt, and did my best to forget him, though with little success. When word came that he was betrothed to Dalla Tostadottir, I grew sick at heart and kept to myself for weeks. One moment I wanted to cover Gisli with kisses, another moment I wanted to force myself on him, and the next I wanted to thrash him till he bled.

8.

THEN CAME THE GREAT COMMUNITY celebration of Yule in Uncle Svein's long hall. Gisli, as handsome as ever, was there with Dalla, a striking redhead, daughter of a prosperous farmer in the district. He kept maneuvering her close to me, as if to show off his conquest and assure me of his normality. We both drank far too much. Then, after midnight, finding the longhouse's latrine occupied, we both ended up staggering outside to piss. Bitterly cold as it was, no one else was around. And I began a conversation that I regret to this day.

Light flurries fell about us. Shaking off my prick, remembering how sweetly it had transfixed Gisli's mouth and arse, I regarded him: so well shaped, so finely featured. I knew in that moment that I would never care so deeply for anyone again and would do anything to possess him. I wanted to beg him to leave Dalla and run away with me, but instead I said, "So when is your marriage?"

Gisli stood half-turned from me, still pissing. In the gleam of the compound's festive torches, steam rose from the snow.

"Come the spring."

"And am I invited?"

Gisli tucked himself in. "No, you are not."

"And why is that?" I took a step toward him. The drunken urge to seize him in my arms, overpower him, and carry him off was immense. I felt half-mad with yearning.

Gisli grimaced. "You know why. Don't pretend you don't. You're always staring at me, Einar. Your attentions are inappropriate."

Gisli headed for the longhouse door, but I blocked his way. "Please, Gisli. Can't we talk?" The pleading in my voice was pathetic, but retaining my pride seemed like a small thing in the face of losing him entirely. "You've avoided me ever since we returned from our summer travels. I think I know why. But what happened on Freysholm, there's no shame in—"

"Shut up, Einar. Someone might hear. I don't want to think about any of that. Let me pass."

"Not yet, battle-brother." Grabbing Gisli by the arm, I dragged him across the snowy garth toward a nearby outbuilding. He gave me only a little resistance, cursing me beneath his breath. I had counted on his fear of attracting witnesses to keep him quiet, and I had judged rightly. Soon I'd shoved him into the building.

"Don't you miss what we shared?" I grabbed his arm in the darkness, but he shook me off. "Did you not find it as wondrous as I?"

"No. I want to forget it. If people knew, we'd be ruined."

"Probably. But that's no reason to turn our backs on something so god-sent." Seizing him by the shoulders, I pushed him back against the wall and kissed him.

For a few seconds he didn't fight me. Hope began to well in my breast, but then he pulled away.

"Damn you. You're a fool, Einar. If anyone found out that you'd forced me that way—"

"Forced you? Your memory deceives you. I didn't force you. I asked you for that boon, and you willingly gave it."

"You held me down. You put your hand over my mouth. You forced me. You unmanned me!"

"Unmanned you? And what is the definition of a man, Gisli? A prick first, yes? And you were stroking your prick as my prick pounded you. Two pricks, there's nothing womanly about that. That's doubled manliness, my friend."

"That's not how others would think. If you ever told anyone—"

"To Hel with others. May Her dark world swallow up those who disapprove. And what else makes a man? Strength and courage? You have those aplenty. But loyalty? That you lack."

Again I shoved him back against the wall. Emboldened with many a drinking horn of ale, I kneaded his crotch and rump. "How could you give me the gifts of your beautiful body—your thick, sap-drooling prick and your furry, so-tight arse—and then turn from me so completely? How could you? Please, Gisli, touch me. I love you, man. Please give me—"

My words ended abruptly as Gisli kneed me in the groin. I gasped, swayed, and slumped over in agony.

"You're a pervert, Einar. A sad, unnatural beast. Weak and womanly. I'm betrothed. Stay away from me, or you'll regret it."

With that, he strode off through the snow toward the sounds of continuing festivity.

9.

IT WAS THE WEEK AFTER Gisli's spring wedding to Dalla that word came to my family's farm that my former friend was reciting slanderous verses about me. The poems, it was said, contained such incendiary phrases as "cock-feaster," "stallion-sucker," "arse-eater," "prick-thrall," and "aching famine of the hero's butt-hole." In any other circumstance, I might have been amused.

I knew why Gisli was doing what he was. Marrying Dalla was one way he might ensure that his manhood was beyond question. Blackening my reputation was another. Such a move would protect him if his worst fear were ever realized, if ever I told someone of taking him in the rear. He'd forestalled any accusations of his own unmanliness by accusing me of the same.

The poems were bad enough. Then came worse news. Gisli had erected a scorn-pole at a distant crossroads. My mother and brother were horrified. I was simply enraged.

I had to see for myself, and so I set off. What the rumors claimed was true. The carving was well done. Anyone who knew me would recognize me as the object of the image. It represented me on my hands and knees, grinning like an idiot, with a huge-cocked stallion behind me, its member impaling my bum. One unwise passerby who hooted at me soon regretted the size of my fists. After I'd dealt with that fool, I tore the scorn-pole down.

I could have brought charges of slander against Gisli. Instead, the next afternoon I was waiting for my former friend near the docks, where he was due to join his fellow fishermen. I gave him time for neither apologies nor explanations. A crowd of people watched in shocked silence as I beat him up. I split his lip, blackened his eyes, and punched him in the gut twice. Afterwards, I licked his blood from my hands, left him groaning on the ground, and headed down the dock to seek passage for Norway.

10.

COUSIN SNORRI'S GRAVE-CAIRN IS SO new it has grown little grass yet. I kneel down before it and touch the stones. As children, Snorri and I spent a lot of time in one another's company—working the farms, fishing, playing games—since our fathers were brothers and lived not very far apart. He'd had red hair like his father Svein, a lean figure, and a real talent with the bow and arrow.

What could have happened between Gisli and him? When I was fifteen, I attended Snorri's wedding to Gisli's sister Steingerd. Gisli always claimed to be fond of his brother-in-law. How could Snorri have enraged Gisli so badly that Gisli could have stabbed him and mutilated him in such a shameful manner?

I have little choice. Gisli was my companion for only a year. He was something more—much more—for three nights before our travels ended and he turned his back on me. He's stridden naked through my night-dreams and daydreams ever since, wherever I roamed: England, Norway, Miklagard. But Cousin Snorri I knew since I was a child, and Gisli dealt him a treacherous blow and a wretched end. Every Icelander knows that an honorable man must avenge a kinsman's death.

I mount my stallion Kolfaxi, a strong black beast lent me by my brother, and head down the grassy slope towards Svein's longhouse. I find him in the pasture beyond, watching a thrall feed mares grain.

"Einar. Good to see you. Aren't these animals grand?"

"They are, sir," I say, dismounting. Uncle Svein has always been wealthy, though not particularly generous. Only his hatred for his son's slayer made that bag of silver bulge so.

"Have you decided?" Svein's hand falls on my shoulder and gives it a familial squeeze. "Are you ready to do your duty? Will you punish your kin's killer and reap the rewards?"

"Yes, uncle. I loved Gisli as a friend, but I loved Snorri as family. Family outweighs friendship. So, yes, I will accept your deal. I will track down Gisli, as much to help Thorstein with his debts as to bring you the justice you seek. But, because of the mutual fondness Gisli and I shared in the past, though that feeling is long dead, I will not slay him unless it's absolutely necessary. I will subdue him, and then I will bring him to you."

Svein smiles. "That will be sufficient. Better, perhaps. It will give me the pleasure of slaying him with my own hands. After the foul way he murdered and maimed my son…perhaps he'll meet the same fate."

I imagine the soft-fuzzed bollocks I lapped between Gisli's legs, then imagine Svein's dagger severing them. It takes all my self-control not to grimace and wince. If Gisli must die for his crime, better that he be given a swift death. Perhaps it would be preferable if someone who once cared for him finished him. Perhaps, once I have captured him, I will let him decide.

"So, nephew, have you any idea where he might have taken refuge?"

"No, sir. We ranged all over the country that summer."

"See my sister. Aud is a priestess of Freya. She's trained in the old sorcery, and she can see things most of us can't. If anyone can help you find Gisli, Aud can. As you know, she lives only a few valleys to the east."

"A fine idea, sir," I say. Indeed. Aunt Aud helped me understand many things when I was a youth, and much she predicted has come to pass. Her knowledge might lead me to Gisli, though my reunion with him will not be of the sort I'd hoped for for so many years. His long-ago slandering of me I might have come to forgive, but not his savage actions against my family.

"Spend the night, nephew," Svein says. "We'll have a feast to seal our deal. Roast lamb, perhaps. Then tomorrow you can consult Aud. Many is the time I've been thankful that we have a sorceress in the family."

11.

AUNT AUD IS WAITING FOR me in the door of her sod-covered hut when I ride up. She's nearly my height, very tall for a woman, with a strong jaw and brown hair gone mostly gray. She's wearing long black robes and carrying a staff, the customary garb of the Vanir priesthood.

"I've been expecting you, nephew," she says with a warm smile.

"Another vision?" I ask, dismounting.

"Not at all. Svein told me you'd be visiting. It's so good to see you after all those years you spent abroad. You've grown into quite the magnificent man. Your father would be proud. Come inside and let's have some breakfast."

Over barley porridge and creamy *skyr*, we exchange small talk about our family's affairs, local gossip, and my overseas adventures. In the center of the hut, a turf fire burns.

"Let's walk," Aud says, rising. "It's a fine day, and I'd like to stretch my limbs."

I follow her outside. She may be nearing old age, but her stride is as long as mine. We make our way up the rocky hill behind her hut. From its slope, we can see much of the region: green grasslands to the south, stretching to the sea, and lava fields to the north, ascending into mountains and perpetual ice. I can feel the cold breath of the distant glacier on my cheek, as if it were kissing me from afar or allotting me some special doom.

At the top of the hill sits a flat rock, like a natural altar. Upon its cushions of grayish-white moss, my aunt and I sit.

"This hill is Freyafell," she explains, "where I come to see far, in both this realm and the next. One of many entrances to the Other World is here. When it is time for me to die, it will open, and I will step inside to join our ancestors. So, you have chosen to help Brother Svein find Gisli Bjornsson, as your family duty dictates."

"Yes, I have, though I'm less than eager. Gisli and I were good friends for a time."

"I know that. There is a special connection between you two. Your fates are intertwined. I know this, for I have had visions to that effect. There are several things I must tell you, and the first is that it is your destiny, your *wyrd*, to track down Gisli. The three Norns decided that on the day you were born, nephew."

I prop my chin in my hands and sigh. "I accept that. But must he die?"

"Do you not wish to slay him, after what he did to Snorri? After how he tried to shame you so long ago? You are no stranger to killing, Einar. On how many raids have you gone? Did you sweet-talk the people of Northumbria out of their possessions?" Her harsh chuckle sounds like her brother Svein's, or my father's when he was in one of his darkly ironic moods.

"I am a warrior. I have killed many a man, yes. And I regret none of it. But none of them were men I cared for. Are we sure that Gisli slew Snorri and mutilated him? Gisli slandered me, true, but he was never the sort of vicious man who might—"

"The law council examined the evidence and pronounced him guilty. If he is innocent, I cannot see it. I only know you must pursue him. And you must capture him. That is your fate. Whether you end his life or bring him to Svein for punishment, I do not know."

"Then I will leave tomorrow. But where do I go? Uncle Svein said that you could help me find him."

"Tonight, a dream will give you the direction your path must take. When I cast the rune staves this morning, *Ehwaz* and *Kenaz* were prominent. The first announced travel, perhaps over water. The second announced fire, which I take to be the passion of revenge, the flames of justice devouring the wrongdoer. Perhaps Gisli will be burnt to death."

"Not by me. If I must kill him, I'll make it swift and simply run him through." I pat the pommel of my sword. "What else have you seen, aunt?"

"Two other things. After you capture Gisli, you must not allow him to speak. Stop his mouth, or slay him posthaste. If you let him speak, somehow your mission will fail. He will have power over you. And you will be forced to leave Iceland forever."

"What? How strange. Why is that?"

"I'm not sure. Perhaps his words are dangerous. I've heard he comes from a line of sorcerers and skalds who were said to have the ability to enchant their listeners."

"Yes, that's true. When we were friends, he boasted of having a forebear who cursed a chieftain."

"Perhaps he has the same gifts. Beware then."

Aud runs a hand over the gray moss, then rises. I follow her down the slope.

Halfway down, she pauses. "One last thing. Somehow the gods are involved. You will see omens in a moment of confusion, and the nature of those omens will tell you what to do. They're likely to be animals. Odin's raven, perhaps. Or one of the beasts that pull the chariots of the gods. Thor's goat? Frey's boar? Freya's cat, perhaps." Aud shakes her head. "That's all I see. I don't think you're meant to know more. More knowledge at this point might somehow lead you astray."

12.

I SPEND ANOTHER EVENING ENJOYING my uncle's hospitality, devouring an assortment of roast meat, cheeses, and brown bread alongside copious amounts of ale. Politely I avoid the attentions of a bold bondswoman who seems intent on flirting with me. When Svein asks me about my visit to Aunt Aud, I give him vague answers, somehow afraid that revealing the details of Aud's advice might be unlucky.

The household goes to bed late. Curled drunkenly into my blanket by the long fire, I slip into one of my customary fantasies about Gisli's naked body. Guiltily, I drop my prick when I realize that I'm sleeping in the house of a man robbed of his only son by Gisli's actions. Rolling closer to the fire, I try to sleep.

In the morning, I wake early, bladder full and head throbbing from the aftermath of too much drink. I stagger to the latrine to relieve myself and am in mid-piss when I remember the dream that Aud had promised would come.

After breakfast, I pack my bags with provisions and mount up. Svein gives me travel money and sees me off. I claim to be heading to Tunga, where Gisli and I spent a few weeks helping in the hay harvest, but actually I am riding toward the West Fjords. Why I feel compelled to conceal the truth from my uncle, I don't know.

While I ride, I recall the details of my dream. Gisli was bathing in hot springs, very far from here. His nakedness was more glorious than ever, but his face was older, drawn with care. The wind was strong, ruffling high grass. Surf boomed, the moon glittered on the water, and the *tjaldur* piped its haunting call.

He is on the island of Freysholm. Why he would return to a place where I unmanned him, as he put it, I do not know. I only know I must go there.

13.

THE TRIP TAKES DAYS. I stay with a series of farmers, paying my way with Svein's money. I get into a brawl with an ill-mannered thrall. I wait out a summer deluge in a barn. I ask about Gisli and am told by several folks that a man fitting his description came this way in May, right after the time of Gisli's sentence to full outlawry.

"He had a sharp tongue," reports an old man near Saurbaer. "He spoke a foul poem against me when I told him I had no food to spare."

I continue toward the island, more convinced than ever that I'm on the right path. Every night, I dream of Gisli. He's thin, dirty, grim-faced. Sometimes he stares out to sea, with tears coursing down his cheeks.

On the eighth day, my horse Kolfaxi trots over a rise and the island of Freysholm comes into view. I dismount in the garth of a farmhouse near the sea. A man with a huge gray beard shambles out of the animal shed to meet me. He regards me with suspicion.

"Good evening," I say. "Might you watch after my horse for a night? I'd be glad to pay."

His suspicious expression shifts into enthusiastic greed. "I could do that, sir. Most certainly. What's your business here?"

"I'm searching for a man, and I think he might be on Freysholm."

The old man's face creases up. "Freysholm? I wouldn't go there. It's crawling with dark elves. It has since time out of mind. It's a place of strange enchantment. Men lose their senses there, it is said, and are never the same."

I nearly laugh out loud. "So has been my experience," I want to say. Instead, I pat the Thor's hammer pendant upon my breast, then the sheath of my sword. "The Thunder God will protect me, as will my own right arm. Have you seen any signs of human habitation on the island?"

"Men rarely go over there, due to the elves. But I have seen the smoke of a fire on some days. Whom do you seek?"

"An outlaw from my district. Have you a boat I could rent?"

Within the hour, I shove my small craft off the strand, climb in, and row toward the island in dim summer dusk.

14.

FREYSHOLM IS SURROUNDED ALMOST ENTIRELY by steep cliffs. As I well remember, only to the southeast is there a beach. I drag my boat up onto the shingle, then ascend the narrow path that winds sun-wise up to the windswept top. The view is immense, taking in the hills of the mainland to the east and the silvery stretch of twilight waters to the west. Carrying a pack of provisions, I make my way toward the island's center. Located there is the dell where Gisli and I spent those nights together so long ago. Even from this distance, I can see the glow of a fire.

There are no trees on Freysholm, only a few ragged shrubs and high grass seething in incessant sea wind, but there are boulders aplenty to shield me from sight. I make my way closer and closer, past the rising steam of hot springs, till I am able to peer over an outcropping and spy on the little campsite. I never doubted Aud's words or the accuracy of my dreams, but I nearly gasp nevertheless, seeing Gisli Bjornsson for the first time in nearly ten years.

The outlaw's hunkered down by the fire, poking embers with a stick. He's naked to the waist, wearing only tattered trousers and dirty boots. His hair's shaggy, falling over his shoulders, and his golden beard's full and unkempt. He's filled out—thicker-built all over, more muscular than I remember. This is not the boy I beat up so easily on the docks. This man might actually give me some trouble.

I study my erstwhile companion's beefy shoulders, biceps, and chest, my throat dry and my blood racing. I should simply be sizing him up and contemplating my next move, but the outward evidence of his strength—and well I know that the greater his strength, the greater a danger he might pose—his unclothed musculature makes my cock stir nonetheless. The boy I knew and loved, the boy I grappled with so passionately in this very dell, was a splendor. This man is even more magnificent. The thought of destroying such beauty makes my gut clench, despite all he's done.

Well, I have my duty. Aud told me that capturing Gisli was my fate. I have no byrnie or helmet, so the safest, the easiest way to take him would be to wait till he's fallen asleep and then press the point of my sword against the pit of his neck. But I savor action and battle too much for that. I want the pleasure of overpowering him, of showing him—he who kneed me in the balls and called me a weak nithing— that I am the better man. He may be burlier than he used to be, but I have no doubt whatsoever that I am mightier.

And so I drop my pack, take up my shield, and step out into the firelight. "Here we are again, little man," I say. "The Norns must have wished it so."

Gisli's spun from the fire and snatched up his shield and sheathed sword before I've taken another two paces. Yes, well, he always was much faster than I. I'll have to take that into consideration.

"What do you want?" Gisli snarls. He has his weapon half-pulled before he recognizes me.

"By Odin. Einar? Is that you?" He brushes a lock of hair from his eyes and stares at me.

"Yes, battle-brother. Back from many adventures."

"Why—why are you here? How did you find me?"

"A dream found you for me. I'm here for my uncle, Svein Ketilsson." I move closer. "He hired me to find you."

"Oh, no." Panic floods Gisli's face as he unsheathes his blade. It's the dragon-pommeled sword I remember from our time before.

"Yes. I mean to take you back to him. Shall you go willingly, or must we decide this with violence?"

Gisli backs up, putting the fire between us. "I'm not going back with you, Einar. Svein will slaughter me like a sheep. You know that."

"I do, and I regret it. But after what you did to Snorri, I have our family honor to uphold. Do you deny slaying Snorri?"

Gisli hesitates. "Snorri deserved to die. Believe me. He was a pig."

I sigh. "I had hoped that there might be some mistake, but now I see that the law assembly was right in its decision. Come with me, Gisli. Surrender, and I won't harm you."

"No, Einar, please. In the name of our former friendship—"

"Friendship?" I snarl. "It was more than friendship. I loved you. But you wanted none of it. You insulted me. You did your best to humiliate me. You sang your nasty verses and erected that fucking scorn-pole. You made Iceland intolerable for me. Now be silent and lay down your weapon. You have no chance against a warrior of my abilities."

Gisli scowls. "I'm going nowhere without a fight."

"I was hoping you'd say that." I pull my sword and charge him with a hoarse roar.

Gisli parries my blow with his shield. He swings at me. He's agile and he's quick; the very tip of his sword catches me on the brow. I stagger backward, wishing I'd bought a new helmet. Blood pours into my eyes, veiling my vision. Cursing, I wipe it away, then slash at him. I cut him across his bare breast, but the wound must not be deep, for it barely slows him down.

His sword crashes into my shield, nearly cleaving it. I return his blow in kind, splitting his shield in half. He flings it away in disgust. Determined to make this a fair fight, I throw my shield away as well.

For another half a minute, we're swinging and dodging, snarling and thrusting. Then I grip my sword with both hands and slam it down against his blade with all my might.

Gisli's sword shatters. He holds up the useless hilt, staring at it in wild-eyed shock. Then he throws it to the ground and, howling, tackles me.

I drop my sword and seize him, trying to pin his arms to his sides. We roll about on the grass for only a few seconds before I've used my greater brawn to force him onto his back.

"Enough," I spit, punching him in the jaw. His head snaps back, meeting exposed rock with a dull thud. He stares up at me with a second's surprise before passing out.

15.

THE FUR PLASTERING GISLI'S CHEST-MOUNDS and belly-plain is red-gold with blood, but bandaging can come later. Now, before he comes to, I must bind him, and bind him well. He must not escape.

Fetching rope from my pack, I tie his wrists behind him, then secure his arms to his sides with cords I knot around his biceps and chest. Tomorrow we will travel, but not tonight, and so I bind his feet together as well. Finally, remembering Aunt Aud's warning, I stuff his mouth with a rag and tie it in place with a few feet of rope pulled between his teeth and wrapped around his head.

When he's restrained and silenced to my satisfaction, I wipe blood from my eyes and cup up water from the hot springs nearby. I wash and bandage my forehead. Then I tend to the wound I inflicted on Gisli, a very shallow cut across his left pectoral that I clean and swathe with cloth. Once I made love to his body, and now my duty has driven me to damage it.

Weary and rueful, I add sticks to the fire, lie beside Gisli on the blanket, and let my eyes rove over him. My hand, as if under the direction of an unseen spirit, rests on his chest. I fondle the silky flesh of a nipple, the ridges of his ribs, his hair-rimmed navel. I finger-comb his messy beard. I rest the palm of my hand upon his breast, close my eyes, and feel the slow throbbing of his heart. After all these years, I still carry inside me that useless and ill-fated love for him, an ardor against all reason or duty.

Cursing my foolishness, I pull my own blanket from my pack, cover myself, and watch the stars wheeling overhead. Somewhere, another *tjaldur* bird gives its eldritch call. Why was I allotted this *wyrd*, to love a dishonorable man, a killer of my kin? Heartsick, I listen to the sea and wait for my captive to regain his senses.

16.

I WAKE TO A SHARP blow against my shin and the sound of muffled shouting. The sun's risen, and Gisli's thrashing about. He's kicking at me as best he can. His heel catches me again in the shin.

"Damn you." I rub my leg, then roll over on top of him. His blue eyes are wide and glaring. Bellowing, he gnashes his gag and tries to knee me in the crotch. I trap his legs between mine, grip him by the shoulders, and shake him.

"Shut up, little man," I say. I try to sound stern in order not to feel sheepish, for his bare-chested struggles beneath me are already triggering a stiff sex. Nearly a decade has passed, and yet my body responds to his in exactly the same way it did before. I've often savored the power my considerable strength has given me over most men, and today is no exception: Gisli's present state of abject helplessness makes the situation even more satisfying. He spurned me and mocked me, and now he's under my control, his life in my hands. "Shut up and be still, or I'll make you pay."

When Gisli keeps struggling and shouting, I give him a sharp punch in the jaw, then a second. His eyes roll back, his head lolls, his eyes clamp shut. Just about the time I think he's passed out again, he groans, shaking his head as if trying to throw off dizziness.

"You asked for that," I say, rolling off him and getting to my feet. "If you want more of the same, keep fighting me and I'll be glad to beat you senseless. If you don't, behave and I'll get us some breakfast. All right?"

Gisli glowers. He rolls over, his back to me. He lies there in silence, wrists working futilely against their encircling rope, as I open my pack and get out cloth-wrapped food: dried meat, cheese, and bread. I pull out my hip-dagger and halve it all.

"It's ready. Roll over."

Gisli obeys. The anger in his eyes has been replaced by desperation, which mingles with fear at the sight of my long knife. The mumbles he makes against his gag are, I have no doubt, pleas for mercy.

"No, I'm not going to stab you. I'm not going to unbind you, either. We're heading home today. You have no choice in this matter. The only decisions left to you are whether to prove difficult and suffer my wrath or be obedient and be treated as kindly as my many grudges against you will allow."

I lift the dagger and run my thumb along its sharp edge. "A seeress told me that I should not allow you to speak once I had made you my captive. That seemed like wise advice, since you yourself once boasted to me that your ancestors were adept at cursing. I won't risk exposing myself to your sorceries. So…I will feed you now, as long as you promise not to speak. If you do start to speak, I might feel obliged to cut your throat. Do you promise?"

Gisli bows his head and stares at the grass. He flexes, his big arms bulging, the tight bonds cutting faint furrows into his flesh.

"Fight the ropes all you want. You aren't getting loose. I've had a lot of practice subduing captives in my adventures overseas. So, what is it? Starvation? Or silence? Will you keep silent?"

Gisli strains against his restraints once more, then falls still. He nods.

"Good," I say, sliding the flat of the blade across his windpipe. "Just remember, I'll shut you up if I have to. Maybe for good."

When I unknot the rope between his teeth and pull out the spit-soaked rag, Gisli does indeed keep silent. I feed him breakfast with my fingers, then gag him again before eating my own portion.

"I need to relieve myself. You do too, I'd imagine?"

Gisli's face flushes. He nods. I free his feet. Gripping him by the elbows, I help him stand. His earlier struggles must have disturbed his wound, for a few trickles of half-clotted blood stripe his side. I wipe the sticky red up with the back of my hand, then lick it off.

I lead him over to the spring. There, I take advantage of his need, touching him in intimate places I haven't seen or felt since we were last here so many summers ago. I pull his trousers down, hold his prick while he pisses, steady him while he squats and shits, clean him up with warm water and moss, then relieve myself in the same ways before washing my hands in the spring.

I smother what remains of the fire and pack up what few belongings of his I find: a blanket, a shirt, a bow and some arrows, dried fish, the shattered fragments of his sword. How he could have subsisted here for so many weeks with so little is a mystery.

"Time to go," I say, looking over the dell where we'd first made love, a time of happiness I'm sure never to see again. Turning to my prisoner, I squeeze his bare shoulders—dense muscles beneath such soft skin—and for a long moment gaze into his summer-sky eyes.

"You're such a handsome man, Gisli Bjornsson," I sigh. "We could have been blood brothers. Somewhere, somehow, we might have had a life together."

I know I shouldn't, but I can't stop myself. Leaning closer, I nuzzle the jaw my fist bruised. It takes all the willpower I have left not to kiss his rope-distorted mouth.

"Why did you have to destroy what we had? Why did you have to murder Snorri? Why did you have to ruin all my hopes?"

Gisli grimaces. He blinks his long yellow lashes at me. Pain floods his gaze, pain so deep I think he might weep. Instead, he turns from me and looks out to sea, where gray clouds are crowding the horizon.

I clear my throat, remembering my duty and his crime. "Bad weather coming in from the west," I say. "We'd better get to the mainland as soon as we can." Gripping him by the arm, I guide him away from the fire-pit's wet ashes and onto the path leading to the beach.

17.

GISLI LEANS AGAINST THE WALL of the shed as I pay the old crofter what I owe him, plus a few extra coins for dried meat and berries. A couple of farmworkers stand in the door to the animal shed, staring at my captive. No doubt having witnesses to his half-naked, trussed-up humiliation is a bitter thing for him. His blue eyes vacillate between smoldering rage and blank despair.

Kolfaxi is led out, looking plump and well cared for. I loop rope around Gisli's neck, then mount up, thank the farmer, and lead my captive out of the garth and onto the road. With Gisli on foot, the way home will take twice as long, but I'm in no hurry. Delivering him into Uncle Svein's hands will not be pleasant.

Other than a mid-afternoon stop by a mountain spring, where I wash our wounds and change our bandages, we travel without pause.

Above us, thickening clouds threaten rain. The road twists among windy pastures, the shattered gray of lava fields, across narrow bridges spanning burbling streams, past a few scattered farmsteads, and between looming hills. We meet no one all day.

Gisli stumbles every now and then but doesn't dawdle behind. He keeps a good pace beside me, as if it were a point of pride, most likely the last expression of pride his life has left. He shoots me frequent glares of resentment. More often than not, he strains against his bonds, trying to wriggle free. Loki-clever as he is, I suspect it'll be a challenge to keep him tied, so I'll have to watch him closely all the way home. Fortunately, I can hardly keep my eyes off his bare, bound-up torso, so for once duty and pleasure converge.

The setting sun's broken through clouds when we come to a prosperous-looking longhouse surrounded by an unusually large number of outbuildings. From the looks of it, it's the compound of a chieftain. As I dismount, a young male thrall with a dirt-streaked face hurries over to greet me.

"May I help you, sir?" He studies my bruised and bandaged prisoner with obvious anxiety. Gisli, exhausted after the long day's travel, drops to his knees, then slumps down onto the ground and rolls onto his side. He grits his teeth, glares at me, groans, and closes his eyes.

"I'm looking for lodgings for the night," I reply, adjusting the strip of cloth wrapped around my wounded brow. "I've captured an outlaw and am making my way back south. Who lives here?"

"Egil Hallfredson. Let me see what he says." The thrall runs into the longhouse and almost immediately returns, his face apprehensive. That's an expression I recognize: the look folks give a very large man when they're about to tell him something they know he won't want to hear.

"I'm sorry, sir. My master thinks that allowing an outlaw into the house might be bad luck. But he'll provide you with a meal if you're willing to stay in that little hut tonight." He points to a sod structure that backs up into the side of a knoll. "I've slept there before. It's cozy and clean. There's a cool wind coming up, so I'll make you a fire."

"That's fine." The thought of making small talk with strangers around their long fire doesn't much appeal to me, but the solitude of the sod hut does. The closer we move toward Gisli's doom, the sadder I'm feeling. I need to drink tonight. "Bring the food when it's ready. And some ale, please. I've got travel-dust on my tongue."

18.

"You'll heal well," I say. Gisli sits beside me on the bench as I clean his breast-wound yet again. "It'll make a manly scar." As if he's likely to live long enough for scar tissue to form. He'll be castrated and dumped into the sea by this time next week, that's my guess.

Gisli hangs his head. After hours of transfixing me with angry, guilt-inducing looks, he seems to have run out of them. Instead, his eyes are sad, almost meek. He keeps still as I re-bandage him. The little murmurs he's making sound like gratitude.

The farm-thrall appears, precariously balancing a fragrant tray and three flagons. "Here's dinner and drink. I'll bring you more food in the morning." He gives Gisli a frightened glance before hurrying out.

I unsheathe my dagger. With its blade, I pat Gisli's thick-whiskered chin. "As I said this morning, your two options are starvation or silence. Promise to keep quiet, and I'll feed you again."

"Umm," Gisli grunts, nodding agreement. I loosen the rope between his teeth and pull the rag from his mouth. For a long time, the only sounds are the crackling of flames and the soughing of rising wind, while we share a flagon of ale, a tasty piece of roast pork, and some boiled cabbage and turnips.

"Food's good."

Gisli nods.

"More ale?"

"Umm huh."

I hold the flagon to his lips. He gulps and gulps and gulps.

"You pig. Don't drink all of it," I say, jerking the flagon away. Foamy ale spills over his lips, bedews his beard, dribbles down his furry chest, and stains his bandage. I fight back the urge to kiss this killer of my kin and to lick ale from his broad breast. Why must what

I want to do and what I ought to do be so damnably far apart? Are the gods dedicated to making men miserable?

Gisli gives me a wry smile. I suspect he'd be saying "Fuck you, battle-brother" if my dagger weren't so near.

"Let's get some sleep." Bunching up the wet rag in my hand, I'm about to gag him again when he whispers, "I think I understand how you feel."

I'm so surprised by the gentle tone of his voice that I pause.

"You do?" I know I shouldn't allow him further speech, but something about his deep, calm voice seizes me. He's not lying, I'm sure of it. He's being honest.

"I do." Gisli's lips tremble. "I'm so sorry, Einar. So sorry for all of it."

The warmth, love, and tenderness that seethe in my chest…the sudden sense of sick doubt I feel…these feelings could be enchantment. He could be trying to cast a spell on me. Aunt Aud warned me. Why should I listen to a killer's words?

"You should be sorry." My fear makes me rougher than necessary as I stuff the rag back in Gisli's mouth and rope it in. I check his bonds next. He's managed to loosen his wrist ropes during today's travel, but I've soon rectified that. He gives me no fight whatsoever as I push him down onto the floor, roll him onto his belly, and bind him further, cinching his wrists and ankles behind his back with a short tether till he's bent double. Such a tight hogtie should ensure that he's unable to escape during the night.

"That'll hold you," I say. I pull off my boots, peel off my clothes, and add fuel to the fire. The thrall was right: this is a cozy, warm space. Leaning back on the bench, I nudge Gisli's belly with my foot before starting in on the second flagon of ale. "You're not going anywhere, are you?"

My captive's only response is a deep groan of discomfort. With difficulty, he shifts onto his side and gazes up at me. In the fire's smoky, erratic flickering, I can't read the emotion on his face. Acceptance of his fate? Blank despair? Icy malice? I look away, up at the fire-hole, around at the carved wooden beams. I take a long swig of ale. When I look at Gisli again, he's still staring at me. The blue gleam in his eyes is unsettling.

"Stop looking at me," I say.

Ever so slowly, Gisli shakes his head. I've robbed him of free movement and speech. His gaze is all he has left.

I've heard tales of sorcerers who use their glance to bend men to their will. Perhaps his eyes are as dangerous as his words, though if that were true, Aunt Aud would most likely have warned me. Still....

"Are you casting a spell on me?" I say, keeping my voice flat.

Gisli does nothing. No grunt. No movement of the head or shrug of the shoulders. Just that clear-sky stare. He's poring over my nakedness as if I were a book he were conning.

It's arousing to be regarded this way, but somehow it's frightening too. I'm afraid, and my fear makes me feel like a fool. He's completely helpless, and I'm a powerful man—few men I've encountered in my travels have matched me. Feeling foolish makes me feel angry. I rise, fetch a rag from my pack, and tie it over his eyes. "There, damn you," I rasp.

Sitting back, I finish the second flagon and start in on the third. My head's growing fuzzy, and my body's full of warm weariness. I pull a blanket over myself, take another mouthful of ale, and let my eyes range over my prisoner. His fur-plastered chest and belly, the trammeled muscles of his arms...it's like looking out over hills and plains covered with golden grain.

Frey and Freya, I am so tired of holding myself back, denying my desires, fighting to retain respectable self-control.

"What a gleaming harvest you are," I sigh, squeezing my crotch. "What a manly catch. Why don't I do what I please with you? Whom would you tell? Who would believe an outlaw?"

Gisli takes a deep breath, holds it, then exhales slowly. Even in this dim light, I can see he's trembling.

"Would you tell?" Reaching down, I stroke his yellow hair.

Gisli shudders violently. He shakes his head. He shakes his head again.

"I touched you on Freysholm. Again and again. And you touched me. In the Yule snows, you told me that you didn't want to remember that. Do you remember now?"

Gisli bites down on his gag-rope and nods.

"That was a long time ago. I've been aching for you ever since, damn you. I've guarded Miklagard. I've sailed all over the North Sea and the Baltic too. I've seen the temple at Uppsala. I've seen the palace of King Haakon the Good. I've sacked monasteries and carried away their bright baubles and burnished treasures. I've seen dawn edging Norway's snowy mountains with red-gold. But you are more of a wonder than any of that. I would have chosen you over all those wanderings. Do you understand me?"

Gisli's beefy limbs tense. The tether between his wrists and ankles goes taut. He heaves a long moan. After so many hours with his hands tied behind him, he must be suffering considerably, and some dark part of me takes deep pleasure in that. Not for me the Christians' new faith, its tonsured eunuchs' forgiveness. Give me the gods of my ancestors, most especially Thor's bravery and might: the thunder's ruthlessness, the lightning's vengeance. The sight of my captive's half-naked, powerful form so completely helpless makes both my heart and my cock swell.

"Do you understand me?" I ask again, adding a harsh edge to my voice. "How much I loved you? How you threw that love away? And how I grew to hate you?"

The fire crackles violently. Outside, a hard wind's whining about the hut. After a long pause, Gisli nods.

"Good, good. I'm glad. By the gods, this is exceptional ale." I swig down the rest. "And now we are here. Wyrd has reunited us. And you are bound to die soon. We are alone. And I am going to possess you now. I am going to touch you wherever and however I please. Do you want me to touch you, Gisli? I promise to bring you pleasure, most likely the last pleasures your fate will permit. Do you want me to touch you?"

The sound Gisli heaves is a long, low moan, as if he were keening for the dead. He strains against his bonds till his limbs are quivering. He slumps against the floor. And then he nods.

That's all the encouragement I need. In a trice, I've slipped off the bench and onto the ground beside him. I wrap an arm around him and pull him to me. I cover his face with ale-drunken kisses: his nose, his bruised jaw, his gagged lips, his brow. Violently, I feast on his chest, sucking his nipples, burying my face in the rich fur there, kneading his pectorals, giving them soft punches, teeth-nipping their hard flesh till he's flinching.

"Beautiful. Beautiful," I sigh. "By the Allfather, you smell and feel and taste so fine."

Moving lower, I lap his hirsute belly and tongue-probe his navel. I shuck his trousers down around his knees, snuffle his crotch-hair, tug his bollocks, squeeze and stroke his prick. Despite his perilous circumstances and no doubt terrifying helplessness, his sex-sword swiftly grows hard in my hand.

Then I do what I did on the island, what I've so often dreamed of since: I take his fat cock into my mouth. It's juicy with arousal. Gripping his buttocks, I nibble his foreskin, lick his prick-shaft, and suck the head till his crotch-fur and my beard are sodden with spit. Whimpering and trembling, he thrusts into me, stuffing my mouth and filling my throat. Reaching up, I capture his nipples between my thumbs and forefingers and tug hard. In another second, his groin's slamming against my face, and I'm gulping down mouthfuls of his copious seed. I may not be a poet, but even I can see irony in the fact that it's bittersweet.

19.

I WAKE TO FIND BLINDFOLDED Gisli curled up in my arms. He's poking me in the belly with his fingers and grunting unintelligibly.

"What is it, damn you?" I say, surly with morning. I don't remember removing the tether between his wrists and ankles, but I must have, because my prisoner's no longer hogtied. Instead, he's stretched out full-length beside me, nestled against my chest beneath the blanket. At least I had the sense to leave his hands and feet bound; otherwise, he'd probably be far from here.

The fire's died down to embers, and the hut's full of damp air. The small sounds I hear outside lead me to believe it's raining.

He pokes my belly again. "Stop tickling me," I order, pulling him closer. "Gods, you're so warm."

I caress his chest, massaging a furry pectoral, trapping a nipple and pinching it. I tug at his beard-bush and kiss his white shoulders. When I run a fingertip through the hair in his butt-crack, he begins trembling.

"Easy, man," I mutter. "I won't hurt you. I just can't seem to keep my hands off your tits and arse. It's so hard to stop touching you."

I squeeze a plump rump-cheek before rolling over onto my back. I cough up phlegm, spit it into the ashes, rub my eyes, and stretch my limbs. The distant dawn-calls of curlews and *tjaldur* fill me with melancholy and tug me back to the real world of fact and bitter necessity. Soon the thrall will bring us breakfast; soon we must be on our way.

Why can't it always be like this? Gisli was so sweet last night. He appeared to be so willing. He rode my mouth with such ardor, and his seed tasted so good. Why did I have to make him a powerless prisoner to touch him again?

He pokes my belly, more urgently.

"What is it? Ah, you need to piss?"

"Ummm huh."

"Not quite yet." I reach up, fetching my knife off the bench. I press the blade against his throat. He swallows hard.

"Last night, I gulped down your sex-sap, and it was delicious. Now I'm going to fuck your face, my friend. I want you to suck me as sweetly as you did on Freysholm. You're going to drink my seed, and you're going to thank me for it. I'll allow you only those words of gratitude before you're gagged again. If you say anything else, my bewitching, broad-shouldered, blindfolded sorcerer, I'll cut your tongue out. Understand?"

When Gisli nods, I unstop his mouth, push his head against my groin, and shove my sex down his throat. Soon he's sucking me as eagerly as he had on the island, gulping me down as if his life depended on it.

20.

THE ROAD WINDS THROUGH LAVA fields all morning. It drizzles on and off for hours. I pull my cloak about me, while bare-chested Gisli shivers in the wind. He has trouble keeping his footing in the road-mud and falls again and again. By the time we stop for a late-afternoon snack, my prisoner's sodden and filthy, and I'm feeling an unsettling remorse. Only the thought of my cousin Snorri's mutilated body keeps me to my purpose.

Gisli slumps down on a low boulder while I pull food from my pack. I take in the sight of him: rain-limp hair, bloodstained bandage, burly arms and mud-streaked torso straining in the discomfort of his restraints. Even this bedraggled, he's the most desirable man I've ever met. Lust and pity swirl in my breast. After the enforced closeness we've shared over the last two days, the thought of turning Gisli over to Svein is becoming more and more distasteful.

"You look like a ship rat," I say, removing his gag. "Are you hungry?"

He looks up at me and grimaces. "Yes. Very much."

"Do your bonds hurt you?"

"Yes. Very badly. My fingers are ice and my shoulders are fire."

"Small price for your villainies." I feed him dried meat and a hunk of bread.

"Thank you," he mutters, chewing.

I take his roped-up hands in mine. They're very cold. Again pity wells, and wrath fades a whit. "I'm sorry, my man. It's necessary. I can't allow you to escape."

"I won't try to escape, I swear. By all the gods, I swear. Einar, please let me speak further. There are important things I need to say. My sword—"

"No sorceries now." Frowning, I ball up the gag-rag. "It's time you were silenced again."

Gisli shakes his head. "No. Please, Einar, no. Not yet. There are things you must know. I—"

I seize him by the arm and press the cloth to his lips. He resists me, teeth gritted.

"Open your mouth, Gisli. Stop struggling, or I'll have to thrash you."

Staring over my shoulder, he stiffens. "No, Einar!" he blurts. "Look. Look behind you. Look!"

"What slick trick is this?" I sigh. "If you're not an embodiment of Loki, I don't know who is."

I turn. Now I see what he's seeing. Three men on foot are approaching us from the west.

"I think they mean us harm, Einar. Unbind me, I beg of you."

"I'll deal with them," I say, pouching the rag and rope. "Get behind Kolfaxi now."

I push Gisli to my rear, then step forward to meet the strangers. My instincts tell me that they do not possess the friendliest of intentions. From the looks of them, they're not warriors—they don't stride, they shamble—but they all appear to be armed.

"Ho there," says the tallest. He has a sword on his hip.

What unkempt fellows. Escaped thralls? Whoever they are, they're a sorry-looking lot. Clearly dirt-poor, which means they might be desperate and thus without scruple.

"Gentlemen," I say, crossing my arms across my chest. Three against one. I've faced those odds before, but I'm not exactly fond of them. Still, none of them matches me in height or brawn. "How may I help you?"

"Who's that you've got there?" asks another, moving closer. He's bearing an axe. "Why's he all bound up?"

"He's an outlaw who killed my kin," I reply. "I'm taking him home to justice."

"Is there a reward for him?" asks the second, moving to my right.

I know where this is going, damn it. *Thor and Odin*, I pray silently, rubbing my hammer pendant, *give me strength. Help me protect my prisoner and myself.*

"None of your business," I say, patting my sword's hilt.

"I think that means yes," says the third, moving to my left. "We could really do with some reward money." He's carrying a sickle. Now the three have me nearly surrounded.

"We want him," says the first, pulling his sword. "We're going to take him."

"By Thor, you will not take him," I say, unsheathing my own weapon. "You will not."

The one with the sword charges. Bellowing, I block his blow with my blade, knocking his sword from his hand, and smash my left forearm into his face. He falls backward, cursing.

The one with the axe attempts me next. I dodge his blow, then swing my sword into his side. Blood gushes. He falls to his knees, screaming.

The one with the sickle is a mere boy. He steps forward, assesses me, and hesitates.

"Come on, you filthy thrall. Try me." I wipe blood off my blade, chuckling. "Let's see what that ferocious farm implement can do."

"Sir," says the boy, shuffling from side to side, eyes wide. "Perhaps we should not have..." He licks his lips. "Please, let's lay down our weapons and talk about this. Surely we can reach some sort of agreement that might—"

Behind me, sounds occur in rapid succession. Running feet. Gisli's voice shouting my name. The thump of something heavy meeting soil. I swing around, sword raised.

Gisli, still bound, and my first attacker are rolling around in the grass. The stranger's weapon lies nearby on the ground. Both men are cursing wildly.

I comprehend the situation in an instant. While the boy with the sickle tried to distract me, his friend had risen and was about to strike me from behind. Then Gisli must have knocked him down.

Gisli butts his head against the man's chest. Snarling, the man punches Gisli once in the belly and twice in the side of the head before shoving him aside. He rolls over, snatches up his sword, gets to his knees, gets to his feet. He's about to drive the point of his blade into Gisli's chest.

I leap forward and swing as hard as I can. There's an explosion of gore. The man's head sails off, hits the ground, rolls three times, and comes to a stop against a rock.

Snarling, I stride over to the axe-wielder, who lies moaning on the ground, and I run him through. He stiffens, shudders, and expires. When I turn to finish the last of the trio, I can barely make out the boy's silhouette in the distance.

"He'd be a grand champion in running competitions," I say, hauling Gisli to his feet. We're both spattered with the beheaded man's blood.

"Thank you for protecting me," Gisli groans. Wobbly after such vicious blows, he leans against me.

"Thank you. You probably saved my life." I brush muddy hair from his face.

"I couldn't let him kill you," he says simply. "I-I don't suppose you'll find it in your heart to free me now?" His full lips curl into a weak smile, but his long-lashed eyes are hopeless.

"Free you? I'm afraid not."

"I promise not to blast you with the magic of malignant verse."

That sounds like the easy humor he displayed years ago on the island. A perilous compassion swarms my innards. Again I want to kiss him. Instead, mindful of Aud's warnings, I pull the rag and rope from my pouch.

"Please, Einar. If you'd only let me—Uuuummmmfff! Huhhh mmm!"

"No more words, my furry-chested sorcerer," I say, knotting the cord behind his head. "Now where did Kolfaxi run off to? We'd better get out of here, just in case those serfs had companions around." I lead Gisli forward by his neck tether, but he falls to his knees.

"Can't you walk?" I heave him to his feet.

He shakes his head, swaying. His knees buckle.

"Ah, my little man. That bastard's blows have addled you."

Bending, I haul Gilsi over my shoulder. I carry him across the meadow toward Kolfaxi, who, after having bolted at the sound of battle, is cropping grass a good ways off. I heave my captive across the stallion, secure him there with several yards of rope, and cover him with my cloak.

"There's your reward. You ride. I'll walk," I say, patting his arse. So welcome, any excuse to touch him.

Gisli lifts his head, gives me a rope-distorted smile, nods, and passes out.

21.

BY EVENING, THE STREAMS WE pass are high, the rain's falling harder, the dells between the hills are white with mist, and Gisli's regained consciousness. Time to look for shelter. After a few more sodden miles, the smell of smoke alerts me to the presence of a homestead. High on a ridge to the east, I can make out structures in the mist.

It takes a good half hour to climb up to the compound. Shivering, I lead Gisli-burdened Kolfaxi into the garth enclosure and knock on the door of the longhouse. No one responds. Impatient, I knock harder.

A tiny old woman opens the door and peers up at me peevishly. She looks suspicious, but my size and obvious irritation prompt her to be polite. "Yes, sir? Are you seeking the priest? I fear he's not at home. I'm his attendant, Helga."

"Priest? No." I gesture toward the lowering clouds. "The weather's foul. We need shelter." I nod toward Gisli, still bound across Kolfaxi's back. "There are two of us. I have a prisoner I'm taking south for justice."

"You're welcome here. We have several huts for pilgrims to lease." She points along the ridge. "There, beyond the temple, they are. All empty at present. Take your pick."

"Many thanks. I'd be glad to give the household a generous donation in return for your hospitality." I peer at the temple. Its outlines are vague in the thickening fog. "To what god is it dedicated?"

"Frey, sir."

"Ah, a god of great power, as is his sister Freya." Indeed. The deities of lust and love have nigh about wrecked my life.

"May we pray in the temple? I could do with some guidance, and my captive could use some comfort, for he has not yet reconciled himself to his fate. For that matter," I add ruefully, "neither have I."

"You may, sir. Those who run Frey's great temple in Thverá don't allow outlaws to enter in, but we are not as strict. You must leave your weapons outside, however. And remember, Frey is the deliverer of captives. 'His desire is to loosen the fetters of those enchained,' they say. If you want to keep your prisoner, you might think twice about taking him into the sanctuary."

"I'll keep that in mind. We've traveled through mire and mud all day, and we're both filthy. Do you have a bathhouse?"

"Yes, sir. One built over a warm spring. It's on the far side of the last of the huts."

"Excellent." I pull out my purse and count out several coins, then add a couple more. The hag's face lights up.

"Ale and meat would be very welcome. Mead if you have it."

"We do, sir. Which guest hut would you like?"

"The one closest to the springs, I think." I wring rainwater from my beard. "I assume there's fuel for a fire."

"Yes, indeed. I'd be glad to start one for you right now."

Amazing, the power of money to change moods. She's gone from suspicious crone to hospitable innkeeper in only a few minutes. "Good, good. We'll have a bath later tonight. Right now, we'll visit the temple. May I buy some mead so as to make an offering?"

"Most certainly. Mead often wins the god's favor."

"Later, might you bring more mead to our hut? And our supper? We've had a very difficult day."

"With pleasure, sir." Helga rubs the coins between her hands as if warming them. "The priest will be so pleased with this contribution."

"One last thing," I say, thinking of how best to enjoy another night with my captive. "How well-equipped is your kitchen? There's a certain substance I require."

22.

THE TEMPLE'S FAINTLY ILLUMINATED WITH oil lamps that line the walls and a small fire that burns in the ground before the image of Frey. Gisli still seems disoriented, leaning against me as we approach the statue.

It's roughly hewn of wood, with long hair, a pointed helmet, a handsome, bearded face, a muscular frame, and a very large erect phallus.

"By the gods, Gisli," I say. "The Lord Frey very much resembles you."

Gisli shakes his head and grunts with disagreement.

"He does, man. He does. You might almost be Frey's son. Do you want to pray with me? I think it would do both of us good."

Gisli nods. I almost remove his gag. Surely, if his speech has malevolent magic, its power would not work in the god's shrine. But I'm reluctant to take that chance.

Instead, I help my prisoner kneel before the statue, then do so myself. He's swaying again, so I wrap an arm around him.

I pour out mead before the god, then close my eyes and pray.

Lord Frey, god of the fertile earth,
rider of the golden-bristled boar,
Gullinbursti,
lord of peace and pleasure,
king of virility, manly might,
root of all love, deity of desire,
your staff showering the soil
with the seed of fruitfulness,
guide us, we pray thee.
Give us the valor to drive off
our foes, the strength to do
what we must. Lend us
the wisdom to know and accept
our fates. Lead us to the truth,
toward what is right.

For a few minutes, I am silent, waiting for much-needed guidance. I open my eyes, gazing first at the god, then at the smaller version of him, the beautiful, bruised, and bound captive slumped against me. The thought of Gisli being gutted, beheaded, castrated by Svein…it's an insufferable image that has crept into my mind more and more as the miles home have dwindled. With every hour we spend together, I want to keep Gisli with me always and possess him forever, but his crimes have made that impossible, even if he were to want me as he did on Freysholm. Never have my duty and my desire been at such awful odds. Aud said some god would provide me with an omen, something that would tell me what to do, but there is no sign, simply the sound of steady rain and the flicker of the fires.

"Let's have our dinner," I say, getting to my feet and helping Gisli do the same. "And then a bath. I want to scrub that villain's blood off the both of us." I cup Gisli's chin and lift his face to mine. "You've got mud in your hair and beard, little man. I think that——"

I stop mid-sentence. In the firelight, I can make out slow tears trickling down my prisoner's face. Ever since I became his captor, I've managed to keep up some semblance of a stern façade, but I can feel it cracking now, like frost-split stones breaking loose and tumbling down a slope. Even the thought of Snorri's murder is insufficient armor in the face of such bald-faced sorrow.

"Ah, Gisli. Ah, battle-brother, hearth-sharer. How badly I wish things were different. What cruel *wyrd* has brought us here?"

I wrap my arms around him. He presses his wet face against my tunic and bursts into tears. He weeps loudly and profusely for a long time. When I think of what might have been, it takes every bit of self-discipline I have left not to join him in his display of grief. When he's done, I kiss his brow, then lead him out of the temple and into the rain.

23.

OUR RENTED HUT IS TINY but very toasty. We've both grown tipsy on ale and mead, our bellies full of lamb and barley cooked with mushrooms and broth.

"That was delicious, Einar. That old woman is a cook fit for a king."

"Indeed. Time to be silent, sorcerer," I say, gently gagging Gisli again. After several days with rough rope tied between his teeth, my captive's lips and the corners of his mouth are chafed raw. "Thor delivered us today from those ruffians, and Frey has given us this cozy refuge tonight. Let's have our bath now."

Before the fire, I remove our soiled bandages and strip us both, then lead Gisli out into the chilly rain and fog, down the path, and into the bathhouse, a wooden structure built around a hot spring. Our hostess has lit oil lamps and set out towels.

"Very nice," I say, surveying the steamy space. "Uncle Svein's coins have come in mightily handy."

Gisli's response to the mention of my uncle is a shiver. "I'm sorry," I say, squeezing his shoulder. "Look, little man, I have a proposition for you. I know you're in considerable pain after being bound for so long. What if I were to remove the ropes about your wrists and torso? I would tie your feet to ensure that you don't bolt. But then you could stretch out, and I could bathe you with greater ease. As long as you promise to leave your gag as it is and not give me any fight once your hands are free. Is it a deal? Do you swear in the name of Frey?"

Gisli's nod is most vigorous. And so I do as I proposed, untying first the ropes that secure his upper arms and torso, then using them to bind his feet. Next I free his hands. He heaves a series of agonized moans as he stretches out. I rub his chafed-raw wrists, then the bruised furrows his on-and-off-again struggles against the rope have cut into the firm flesh of his biceps and chest.

"Hold onto me," I say. With straining difficulty, he wraps his freed arms around my neck. I lift him into my arms, carry him into the bath, and ease us both down into the bubbling water. Both of us groan with wordless delight.

I clean myself first, pleased to remove the filth of battle and travel. Then I sit back against the side of the bath and pull Gisli between my legs. He leans against me, his back against my chest. Far from resisting my touch or trying to escape, he seems, thank the shining gods, to savor my attentions. Chest tight with happiness, I clean his breast wound, scrub his face, and wash his long blond hair and beard. He flexes his limbs, closes his eyes, and heaves one contented sigh after another. By the time I'm done cleaning him, he's fallen into a near-drowse, and, thanks to his naked closeness, my cock is uncomfortably hard.

"Feel good?"

"Ummmmmmmm," he mumbles, nodding. "Mmmmmm."

"Let's just lie back for a while," I say, stroking his breast. For a long time, we soak there, luxuriating in the warmth, listening to hard rain on the roof. If it were not for the rope about Gisli's ankles and the gag stopping his mouth, we could be two lovers enjoying the bath.

And if we were simply lovers, not captor and captive? Only our present solitude allows such intimacies. I well know the consequences of discovery. Fear of those consequences was surely what caused Gisli to turn from me in the first place.

"What would happen if the wrong person saw us like this, little man? Both of us naked, you nestled in my arms? We'd be denounced as weak effeminates, mocked as cravens. We might even be attacked and driven into the wilderness."

Beneath the water, Gisli, to my surprise, takes my hand. I squeeze it. In this quiet, peaceful place, I could almost pretend that his past slanders and my grim duty to kin were only bitter dreams.

"Fools," I mutter. "The gods know better. The gods know our manhood is true. Frey and Freya bless all love, I have no doubt." I kiss Gisli's cheek and finger his nipples, which immediately stiffen inside my touch. Between his legs, his cock stiffens as well.

"See how your body responds to my caresses? It knows better than you. Why did you doubt what we had? Everything might have been different."

Reaching down, I take Gisli's cock in my hand and stroke it. "Why did I have to ache for you those long years? Why could we not be together like this?" I rub his cockhead with my thumb, tickle his piss-slit with my forefinger, grip his bollocks and tug them tenderly. "Why could we not keep what we found on Freysholm?"

Gisli presses back against me and groans. He prick-prods my palm and grips my thighs. That cruel stranger in the Yuletide cold who mocked and reviled me, who kneed me in the groin, where has he gone? I hardly care. This golden-furred man in my arms seems to welcome my touch, just as that handsome boy on Freysholm did so long ago.

"I can't wait any longer, Gisli," I say, voice husky with lust. I grip his cock harder; with my other hand, I fondle his arse. "I'm going to bind you now, not only because I don't trust you—this acquiescence you display might be a clever ruse—but because your powerlessness delights and arouses me. Then we're going back to the hut. There,

I'm going to take you the way I did on the island, whether you like it or not. I'll take you by force if I must, but I'd prefer that you were willing, as you were on Freysholm. Are you willing?" I say, nibbling his ear. I wrap my arms around him, ready to subdue him if necessary.

Gisli's robbed of words, but he does not need them. In answer, he rubs his arse against my rampant cock and nods.

"Praise Frey," I whisper. Shaking with wonder, gratitude and reverence, I carry him out of the bath. I leave his feet bound, tie his hands behind him, then heave him over my shoulder and hurry out of the bathhouse, eager to begin.

24.

"I WANT YOU TO WANT me inside you," I sigh, stretching Gisli out on a fur blanket beside the fire. I lie on top of him, covering his face and chest with kisses that alternate between rough and tender. Once more I suck his nipples, and he responds with enthusiasm, arching his chest against me. I suck his cock, squeezing his bollocks and kneading his arse-cheeks till he's fucking my face hard, his blond-furred thighs tensing around my head. When he's close, I pull off, only to untie his feet, haul him up onto his knees, and bend him forward over the bench that lines the wall.

I rub my beard over his pale buttocks, then spread them. The crevice between is newly clean, lined with thick golden hair. Bending, I lick and nuzzle his crack, burying my face in that fuzzy vale. I spread his cheeks wider, lap his hole, and work my tongue up into him.

Gisli gasps and shakes, his bound hands clenching. Half mad with long-denied desire, I lap and probe. His hole tastes salty, like brine springs, and sweet, like honey-mead, and musky, like labor-sweat, and bitter, like hoppy ale. Certainly he's as intoxicating as ale, if not more so. I can't get enough of how he feels and smells and tastes.

I eat his arse-hole till his cleft is sopping wet. When I grasp his sex, it's as hard as I've ever felt it.

"I have a surprise for you," I say, reaching for the vial I'd gotten from Helga. I dip a finger into it and smear the liquid over his nether-gate. "It's rapeseed oil. When I took you on Freysholm, I used only spit, and getting screwed seemed to hurt you at first. This should make the hurt less, I think."

I take my time, rubbing and tickling the little entrance that leads into utter bliss. When he seems ready and relaxed, I push my moistened finger inside, first the tip, then the whole length. I probe his channel, find a tiny promontory and massage it. He squirms, emitting a muffled squeal. Spreading his thighs, he pushes his rump back against my hand.

"Like that?" I chuckle, probing harder. I take my time, finger-fucking him steadily until he's whining and his cock's dripping with delight.

"Now, little man? May I take you now?" Bending, I kiss each arse-cheek.

Gisli gives me a gravelly groan. He gazes back at me, blue eyes wide and wet, full of vulnerability. He's never looked at me with such frank need.

"Yes? Tell me. Yes?"

Gisli closes his eyes. He bows his head, cocks his arse, and nods.

"For this boon, I thank the glorious Vanir," I sigh, smearing oil on my sex, then nudging his hole with my cockhead. Overeager, I enter him too roughly, too fast, but I can't help myself, for I've waited for this moment for nearly ten turns of the Sun-Wheel. Beneath me, Gisli whimpers and winces but gives me no resistance. When I'm sheathed inside him entirely, I kiss his white shoulders and stroke his cock till it's stiff again.

"All right, my little man, my golden warrior? May I continue?"

Nodding, Gisli grinds his arse against my groin. I take a deep breath. "Praise Frey," I say again. Wrapping my left arm around his torso and pressing my right hand over his mouth, I commence a rhythmic pounding.

25.

GISLI LEAVES MY SIDE ONCE during the night. He's most likely going to the latrine, but I count the seconds of his absence, ready to pursue him if necessary. To my relief, he soon returns and is once again curled inside my arms.

Come sunrise, I wake to Gisli's gagged lips rubbing my crotch. My sex has cast off sleep before me.

"More, eh? You want me in your mouth?"

Gisli moans and nods, pressing his face against my sex-fur.

"What a treasure, your hunger." Chuckling, I loosen the rope and remove the gag-rag.

His keen mouth gobbles me, as if my flesh were a feast and he were starving. He sucks me hard, grunting and slobbering with submissive fervor, while I hold his head and drive into him, relishing his tight mouth-hole.

Gisli pulls off and rolls onto his back beside me. He licks his lips, a half-crazed look in his eyes. "Einar...I need..."

I run my hand over his chest, then down his flat belly to grip his sex. "By the gods, you're a glory. You're a grandeur. I want to take into memory how you look, how you smell, how you taste, how you feel. I don't want us to be parted. I don't want to take you to my uncle. I want to forget my duty and deny my fate. After having you again—the way you gave yourself to me last night—I can't...I don't know how I can..."

My eyes are growing wet. Ashamed, I wipe them. I kiss Gisli's bushy-bearded chin and rest my head on his soft-furred breast. "Oh, damn it all to Hel. I don't know what to do. I don't want to lose you. But I can't shame my family."

Gisli doesn't beg for mercy. He doesn't beg me to free him. Instead, he does the one thing that embeds him in my heart even more deeply. He rolls away from me, positions himself on his belly, spreads his legs, and lifts his arse in offering.

"Fuck me again, Einar, my burly bear-brother," he says, turning his head toward me with a sad smile. "Please, big man, I'm begging you. Please fuck me again. Please fuck me hard."

I don't think I've ever been so aroused. "And so I shall, beautiful one," I growl, reaching for oil, rope, and rag. "I'm going to gag you tight, grease up your mead-sweet hole, hold you down, and give you the rump-ramming of your life."

26.

BY THE FIRE'S EMBERS, I sweetly ravish Gisli Bjornsson—my prisoner, my battle-brother, my lover, doomed to die. Roaring, once more I spend my seed deep inside him. Afterward, he lies on his belly, eyes closed, a faint smile lingering on his lips. I rise, pull on my trousers, and step outside to see if the rain has stopped.

On the threshold I stand, belly rumbling with hunger. Sunlight glitters in wet grass. I take a few steps into the yard and scan the compound. No witnesses, so I pull out my prick and take a long piss.

I'm barely done, just now pushing my limpness inside my trousers, when something soft rubs across my foot. It's a brindled cat. I bend to scratch its ears. It accepts my affection before prancing off.

I'm about to step back inside when a snuffling sound makes me turn. There, near the bathhouse, is a wild boar. It studies me with dark eyes before rooting in the grass a bit, then trotting away. By the time it disappears around a hummock, I know what I have to do.

When I enter the hut, Gisli's snoring by the fire. He comes awake with a grunt of confusion as I cut his hands free. I cut the cord around his head and pull the wet rag from his mouth. I seize him in my arms and kiss him hard on the lips.

"Einar?" he gasps. Pulling away, he studies my face. "What are you doing? Are you—?"

"I'm freeing you. I can't take you to Svein, no matter what crimes you've committed. I just can't allow you to be killed. I lost you once. I can't lose you again."

"Thank the gods! But what changed your mind?"

"I don't know. Making love to you again. The way you submitted to me and freely gave me the gift of…being inside you the way I've always ached to be. The knowledge that I couldn't live with myself if I performed my duty and delivered you up to Svein. And…and the omens Aud promised me would come, I saw them. Outside…first, Freya's cat. And then Frey's boar."

"Perhaps…obviously I don't want to convince you otherwise, but…perhaps those were simply the compound's animals. Why are you so sure that the gods sent them?"

I laugh. I take his hand. "Because of…how my heart shifted. Aud was right. As soon as I saw them, I knew what I had to do. I knew my true duty."

"Miraculous. By the good gods, miraculous."

"Will you leave, now that I've freed you?"

"Leave? Back to live in solitude and penury on Freysholm? Back to outlawry?"

"Or to Dalla. Your wife."

Gisli's laugh is bitter. "She divorced me long before I was outlawed, big man. Our life together was miserable from the beginning." He lifts my hand to his mouth and kisses the back of it. "No, I'm not leaving. Let's get dressed. We must do something now."

"And what is that? Are you hungry? Shall I fetch you breakfast?"

"I'm famished," says Gisli, "especially after the vigorous exercise you've treated me to." Grinning, he rubs his rump. "However, breakfast can wait. I want to go to Frey's temple to give thanks."

"I too," I say. Rising, I pull him to his feet.

Gisli rubs his rope-burnt wrists and leans his head against my shoulder. "After breakfast, Einar, we must talk. There is much I've been wanting to tell you, much I feared I might never get a chance to say, but thanks to the Shining Ones, today is the day we will share the truth."

27.

HELGA'S TENDING THE OIL LAMPS when we enter the shrine. She looks Gisli up and down. "I told you that Frey loosened the fetters of those enchained," she says. "I'm assuming you're here to give thanks."

"We are, madam," says Gisli, smiling. "The gods have shown me a fate far fairer than that I expected."

"Good, good. Come to the longhouse afterward. I have some tasty cheese and barley-bread, some *bláber* berries and *skyr*-cream."

When she's gone, Gisli takes my hand and leads me to the statue. We stand there in silence and firelight. When Gisli reaches forward and grips the carven cock of the god, I can't help but gasp.

"Come, Einar. Be reverent. Pray with me."

I hesitate, then reach forward. Around the great Frey-prick, our fingers interlock. Gisli lifts his eyes to the god's bearded face and begins a poem-prayer.

> *Golden god, love-lord, sun-bright Frey.*
> *And Lady Freya of gold and amber*
> *Brísingamen, goddess cloaked in*
> *falcon feathers. Odin, Allfather,*
> *gray-eyed wanderer, and red-maned*
> *Thor, whose great thunder-hammer*
> *shatters the wickedness of snow-giants.*
> *All you other powers, Frigga*
> *and Mother Earth, and Loki,*
> *whose tricks twist our hopes,*
> *and the Norns, who weave our fates,*
> *I, Gisli Bjornsson, for my sins*
> *and my stupidity, have suffered*
> *bondage and the death of hope.*

Now Gisli shifts his blue gaze from the god to me. Smiling, he continues.

> *But now my dark-eyed bear-brother,*
> *with his furry breast and beard*
> *black as Irish midnight, and his*
> *great arms, Thor-storm-strong,*
> *and his great prick-sword,*
> *gift of this very god we grip,*
> *Einar has saved us both from*
> *a most bitter doom. Once,*
> *with his matchless strength*
> *he broke my dragon-sword*
> *in which lay my family's fate.*
> *He vanquished me, bound*
> *and silenced me, led my neck-*

tether along sharp, rocky ways
of despair and shattered ice.
With grim purpose he thought just,
he dragged me toward death's cold mere.
Then you Shining Ones heard my prayer.
Through your mercy I am spared.
Now Einar has saved me from that end,
cradling me in hot and healing springs.
Frey's prick-priest, he has thrust me
full of cock-mead seed-sap and joy.
He has cut my bonds, released my words.
Now his will is mine, and fate's sword-
shards and my brimful heart insist
I shall follow him forever.

Gisli's fingertips play over my hand before we simultaneously release our hold on the Frey-prick and step back.

I am almost too stunned to speak. "I, uh, forever? Sword-shards? What do you mean?"

"I will tell you all. Let's have breakfast now. I could eat a whale. Then let's hunt. After so long tied, I'd love to stretch my limbs. You brought my bow and arrows from Freysholm, did you not? I'm sure old Helga would be glad to roast some game-birds for us."

28.

I'D FORGOTTEN WHAT AN AMAZING archer Gisli is. If he'd seen me approaching him on Freysholm the day I captured him, I might have taken an arrow to the heart or head. Then again, I suppose I have. Love for him has transfixed me like a sharp-barbed shaft for nearly half my twenty-five years. Sometimes I feel like snow-gleam Baldur pierced by the mistletoe spear.

We range about the region all day, bringing down ptarmigan. When Gisli's hunting bag is full, we sit side by side on a rocky knoll and share the bottle of ale Helga packed for us, then some smoked fish wrapped in flatbread. Below us, sunlight glints upon a line of small lakes, and curlews sport about, uttering their erratic, quavering calls.

"So speak, man. Tell me what you must."

"I've tried to for days," Gisli says. "But you wouldn't permit me to."

"I'm sorry about that. I already told you why I kept your mouth sealed shut. Well, I liked having you in my power," I admit with a sheepish grin. "It excited me to keep you helpless, to control the movement of your limbs, to rule over your speech and sight."

"I could tell. Tying that rag in my mouth always seemed to get your prick hard. The next time we make love, you're welcome to bind and gag me first. Whatever pleases you will please me."

"Really? Excellent! The thought of that stiffens my sex right now." Chuckling, I pat my crotch and lick my lips in an exaggerated show of lechery. "At any rate, the primary reason I enforced your silence…I told you that on the island. My Aunt Aud is a seeress. She said that if I let you speak, my mission would fail and I would be exiled from Iceland. I was afraid your words had sorcerous power."

"Mighty Einar, afraid?" Gisli nudges my side. "I'm a poet, not a sorcerer."

"Yes, afraid. Don't mock me. But she was wrong. My mission was doomed long before I freed you."

"How so?" Gisli's hand falls on my thigh. How the affectionate, passion-filled boy from our first time on Freysholm has been given back to me, I don't know, but his return is a god-sent boon, the greatest blessing I've ever known.

I squeeze his hand. "There was sorcery, all right. Your sorcery was not in your words, but in your face and form, your beauty. There's been a storm in my chest ever since we first shared our bodies, Gisli Bjornsson. I can never escape you. The gods know how hard I tried to forget you during my many years abroad."

"And I can never escape you, my burly bear. Our parting, the bitterness of it, was entirely my fault. I see that so clearly now. We'll discuss that tonight. But first…your aunt was right. If you'd allowed me to speak, you might have released me days ago. How my speech might cause you to be exiled, that I don't understand."

"So? Tell me!"

Gisli stands. He runs his fingers through his golden hair, then sits back down beside me and begins to braid his beard, as he once did on Freysholm.

"I'll do that," I say, pushing his hands away. "Now talk, for Thor's sake."

"Once so set on shutting me up, now practically begging me to speak." Gisli chuckles, but then his expression turns somber. "Einar, I didn't murder Snorri. My sister—his wife Steingerd—did."

"What?" I gasp and jolt.

"Damn it!" Gisli swats my hands. "You're pulling my beard. Leave off. You're welcome to braid it tonight."

"Steingerd killed my cousin? Steingerd killed her own husband?"

"Yes," Gisli says. Rising again, he begins to pace. "I found her just after she did it. She'd cut his throat and sliced off his balls."

"Uncle Svein told me he'd been castrated. That was one of the reasons I came after you. The insult to my family was just too horrible to forgive."

"I understand. If I believed as you had, I might have done the same thing. After all, you had more than one reason to hate me. Not only had I been convicted of killing your kin, I'd slandered you. I'm sure Svein also tempted you with a great reward."

"He did indeed. It was money that my brother sorely needs to pay his debts. But why did you not tell the truth about the killing? Uncle Svein said that you refused to give a reason for the crime, that you were too poor to pay *weregild*, the compensation for Snorri's life, that you had no kin to help you."

"I had kin. My cousins wouldn't lend me the money because your uncle threatened and intimidated them. As wealthy as he is, he didn't need the *weregild*. He was determined to have me outlawed instead."

"So why did you confess to the crime?"

Gisli kneads his rope-reddened wrists. "Because Steingerd begged me to shield her. She has two children. I was divorced and childless. She had much more to lose than I."

"Do you know why she murdered him?"

"I do. She told me something terrible. She claimed that your cousin Snorri was...forcing himself upon his own six-year-old daughter. When Steingerd caught him at it, she waited till he went to bed, and then she slit his gullet."

"Great Odin." I cover my eyes with my hands. "Raping his own child? And I thought *you* had dishonored my family. I meant to help Svein punish you for Snorri's death, and all the time, my cousin deserved his end. No wonder his wife cut off his bollocks. But why did Steingerd not tell the truth? If she had..."

Gisli snorts. "You know how ruthless and powerful your uncle is. To have his only son accused of such a vile crime? Svein would never have believed it. He would have accused Steingerd of slander. He might have had her murdered."

Gisli stops pacing. He looks out over the gleaming lakes. "Steingerd and I have never been close—she can be vindictive and scheming—but, by the gods, Einar, she's my only sibling. I had no reason to doubt what she said. So I took the blame and fled into the wilderness. After you left Iceland...my life was only a series of sad missteps. I hurt you. I hurt Dalla. Living out in the lava fields and glacial rivers seemed like what I deserved."

Gisli turns. "I thought I'd never see you again. So when I was outlawed, I fled to Freysholm, the site of my greatest happiness: those three days we shared. Then you came for me, seeking vengeance. I thought I was truly doomed. Then, night before last, you touched me as I lay helpless by the fire, and I could feel that, behind your anger, your passion for me remained."

Gisli scans the surrounding landscape. Seeing no witnesses, he wraps his arms around my waist and presses his face against my beard.

"So I prayed to Frey and Freya. I asked to be forgiven for being so foolish, for driving your love away. I prayed that your feelings for me would triumph over your sense of duty, that somehow I would be allowed to speak my truth and beg your forgiveness. Do you forgive me, Einar? I was weak and I was afraid. Tonight, I'll explain everything. I want you to understand why I—"

"Enough, Gisli," I say, pulling him closer. "I forgive you. I think forgiveness began the moment I first touched you again."

"Oh, thank you, Einar! Thank you. And do you want to…be with me? Have a life together somehow? You said once that you loved me. Is that still true?"

"You've felt my hungry mouth on your lips, your breast, your cock, and you've felt my prick pummeling your arse. What do you think?"

"But that might simply be lust, not love. Do you—"

"You just said you were a fool to drive me away. You'd be a worse fool to doubt my feelings now. Yes, Gisli Bjornsson, I love you. Aunt Aud said our fates were intertwined, and she was right. I want us never to part. But what do we do now? My family expects me back. Uncle Svein is waiting, as is my brother Thorstein."

"Can we not head for the nearest port?" Gisli nuzzles my chin. "Take ship somewhere far away? Leave Iceland behind? Start over again?"

"Eventually. Aud mentioned two runes that came up when she threw the future-telling staves. One was *Kenaz*, indicating fire, and that has come to pass, this blessed flame renewed between us. The other was *Ehwaz*, meaning travel. Aud felt it might suggest travel over water."

"My father came from the Orkneys. Perhaps we could go there."

"Funds will be a problem. I fear that I have little money, other than that Svein gave me. And Thorstein's counting on the reward money. I don't want to leave my brother in the lurch."

I pat Gisli's rump and kiss his brow. "We'll figure something out. Let's head back to Frey's compound now. My guess is that old Helga can roast these plump birds to a turn. After supper, let's turn in early. We clearly have much more to discuss."

29.

"You don't need to explain the scorn-pole," I say. "I'm fairly sure I understand."

Gisli and I, both naked, are sitting cross-legged in the bed closet of our little hut. The air is warm with a good long fire that blazes in the earth-hearth. We're sharing a plate of spit-roasted ptarmigan and a huge flagon of ale.

"I want to explain. You know the worst insult one man can fling at another is *sansorðinn*, used like a woman by another man. All my life I've been told that submitting in such a way is contemptible and unmanly. Then there I was on Freysholm, taking great pleasure from your cock driven deep inside me. As soon as we left the island, those voices in my head...voices of condemnation..."

"Others' voices. Not your own?"

"Not my own. But I thought they were then. Einar, I was so ashamed that I couldn't bear to be around you. I wanted you so badly, wanted to feel you inside me again, but for so long I thought my desire for you was an evil thing, like a powerful spirit I couldn't seem to escape. At night, alone, I touched myself, thinking of your nakedness, of your strength, yearning to feel you on top of me."

"I did the same. So often I touched myself, remembering how you looked, how you felt. You don't need to say anything more, little man. I told you: I think I understand."

"No, let me finish. I need to say these things." Gisli takes a long quaff of ale before continuing. "I was terrified someone would discover, so afraid of what others might say. I knew you were angry with me for avoiding you, and I feared you would tell. A few people even teased me about how close you and I had been. Steingerd suggested that folks were saying unseemly things. So—"

"So you slandered me. Before you could be accused of taking it up the rear, you accused me of it. A great stallion shoving itself up my bum! It was well carved, you little bastard." Grinning, I tear roast meat from bone with my teeth. "Poetry, wood-carving, bird-hunting, cock-sucking. You're a man of many skills."

Gisli grins. "As are you. Sword-swinging, kidnapping, arse-ramming. I'm so glad you found me, so glad Frey and Freya led you to me."

"As am I. Sometimes the same doubts plague me, I must admit, those accusations of womanliness. Then I squeeze the muscles of my right arm and the fat member between my legs and count the number of men I've bested in battle, and I come to the conclusion that those who think my desire for other men is unmanly are a pack of dung-beards, dullards, and half-wits."

"Well said. Why did I believe them for so long?"

"Because it's hard to go your own way. It's hard to know what to believe when your heart tells you one thing and everyone around you tells you another. My parents and their beliefs were unusual. Making peace with my unconventional feelings for other men…it was easier for me than most."

"I envy that. The only reason I married Dalla was to forget you. And to banish any doubts about my manhood. That was a huge mistake."

"I'm sure other men have done the same. There have to be other men who feel as we do. In fact, I know there are." I finish my ale and stretch out on the bed, my arms folded behind my head.

"Oh? Have you…had other…lovers?"

"You look surprised."

"I am."

"I was gone for nine years, friend. And I wasn't fighting my desires the way you were. I'm not a eunuch, as some of the silly Christians seem determined to be. There was another Icelander, one in the Miklagard mercenaries with me. A great red-headed brute named Grettir. We spent some nights together."

Gisli frowns. He gnaws a bird leg thoughtfully. "And did you love him?"

"Does it matter?"

"It does."

"Are you jealous?"

"Yes. Yes, I am. I know I drove you away, but still…"

"I didn't love him. Not like I've always loved you. But I was very fond of him. We fought side by side. I was sad when we parted. Sadder when I heard that he drowned when his ship went down in a storm near Sweden. Being with him helped me understand the shame that made you spurn me."

"Oh? How is that?"

"Because, my time with Grettir, that was my turn to be *sansorðinn*. He wouldn't let me fuck him, so I let him fuck me."

Gisli's eyes go wide. "By Odin, is that the truth?"

"Yes. That helped me see why you turned from me, for, despite my upbringing and the freedom of my family's beliefs, I too felt some of that shame. Then I recovered from it, as I would from some annoying sickness. I didn't enjoy getting screwed by Grettir as much as I enjoyed—enjoy—screwing you, but I liked it well enough. It felt good, his big hairy bulk on top of me, pounding away."

I roll over onto my belly, rest my cheek in the bedclothes, close my eyes, and sigh. "If you want to take me that way...if that might make you feel...on the same level of manliness...or requited somehow.... you are welcome. Just go very slowly, and use lots of oil."

Gisli's silent for a long moment. Then his warm hand strokes my arse. "Now?"

"If you'd like," I say, spreading my thighs.

Gilsi swallows so hard I can hear it. "Where's the vial, Einar?" he whispers. "Where did you leave the vial?"

30.

I TAKE MY TURN ON top the next morning, binding and gagging Gisli, sucking his tits into wincing tenderness, then hauling his legs over my shoulders in the very position Grettir used to take me, riding into my golden little man for a hearty, fast fuck. Afterwards, I free him and we curl together, drowsy with satisfaction and bodily bliss. It's raining again, and the *tjaldur* birds are piping and quarrelling outside.

"Einar, that was wonderful. You're a berserker in bed. I love the feeling of your prick inside me," Gisli sighs. "Did you enjoy having me bound again?"

"Gods, yes. Thanks for indulging me."

"Certainly. Screwing you last night was wondrous as well. May we do that again sometime?"

"Most certainly, my man. I want to bring you rapture in as many ways as possible. I wish we could stay in this sanctuary forever, fucking till Ragnarök, but my money's nearly out. We can postpone our fates no longer. We must head home. Otherwise, Svein might send someone after us."

"I suppose," Gisli reluctantly agrees. "After that, with the gods' help, maybe we can find a place no one knows us, where we can start a new life. But what if folks recognize me back home?"

"We'll disguise you. I suspect that, for the right money, old Helga can find you some of the Frey-priest's castaways. Something with a hood to conceal your face."

"Hopefully. As much as I dread getting any closer to your uncle than necessary, I would like to see Steingerd. She must feel guilty for letting me take the blame, and I want to let her know that I'm all right."

"Yes, you should do that. But you must be careful."

"I will, be sure of it. What do you plan on telling your uncle?"

"We still have the shards of your sword, do we not? What if—"

I break off, remembering. "Wait a minute. Your sword. There was something you said in Frey's shrine that you never explained. Something about the dragon-sword and your family's fate, and how the sword-shards would make you follow me forever. What did that mean?"

"Ah, yes. That's the final thing I need to tell you. But first, hold me, Einar, my dark bear. I love it when you wrap me in your arms. You make me feel safe and cherished."

"As long as you have me, safe and cherished you will be."

Gisli rolls over onto his side, his back to me. Embracing him, I pull him closer, then fondle his hairy pectorals, flicking his nipples with my fingernails.

"Easy! I'm sore there, thanks to your feral berserker teeth."

"Good. Next time I'll be even more savage."

"You're a monster," Gisli jokes, snuggling closer. "Abducting me, binding me, torturing and raping me. Possessing me."

"For always, the gods willing," I murmur, probing his navel. "It's you who've possessed me, my man. I've been your heart-thrall, your touch-thrall, for years. Go on now. The dragon-sword?"

"It was passed down to me by my father. Its name is Heart-Biter."

"Appropriate, considering how you've cloven my heart." I pinch a nipple.

"As you have mine. Stop tormenting my chest, damn you. Your new nicknames shall be Einar Arse-Rammer, Breast-Biter, Tit-Chewer."

"And you shall be Gisli Skill-Tongue, Plump-Arse, Fur-Breast. Gisli the Golden Mead-Cup. Continue your story."

"The family legend says that if Heart-Biter is ever broken, the bearer of the sword must swear allegiance to the warrior who shatters it. And so I have. That's why I didn't try to escape my captivity. When I said I'd follow you forever, that's what I meant. I swear my loyalty to you, Einar Eiriksson."

"And I to you," I rasp, heart full and eyes wet. We lie in silence for long moments before I pat Gisli's bare arse and wipe my face.

"What sort of warrior am I?" I growl. "Your magic has brought me near to weeping, my fuzzy enchanter. Enough of these old stories. Let's pack up and be on our way."

31.

My uncle weighs the sword-hilt in his hand, looking dubious. He runs a fingertip along the dragon design.

"Heart-Biter, Gisli said the name was," I say, making a show of adjusting my brow-bandage. "A family heirloom."

Sorcerers might be able to read minds, but I'm glad the common man can't. If Svein knew I had Gisli hidden in a shed back at Thorstein's farm, he'd probably cut out my entrails and feed them to his swine.

"This is all you give me? I wanted the man himself." Svein's face darkens; his brow wrinkles up.

I lean back on the longhouse bench and shrug my shoulders. "I had him. For days I had him, bound and well-gagged as Aunt Aud advised. He was bursting with remorse, I could tell, and riddled with fear of you. We were nearly to this district when we passed a sea-cliff. He broke free of his neck-tether and leaped to his death. Surely you would not wish me to risk my own life by entering the storm-wild sea in order to fish up a corpse? He is dead, uncle, and this sword's fragments are proof of it."

"I have no need of these useless shards." Svein rewraps what's left of Heart-Biter and hands the bundle back to me. "I wanted Gisli Bjornsson. I wanted his body to run through, his head to cut off."

"You wanted him dead. And so he is." I hope I'm being convincing. I've always had much more in the way of Thor-might than Loki-wiles. "So, my reward?"

Svein scratches his chin. "I'm not sure I believe you. Perhaps I should consult Aud. She might be able to see the truth."

Aggh! She well might. I've got to dissemble more adeptly.

"I've told you the truth!" I shout. Standing, I pound a pillar with my fist. "Why would I lie to you? Gisli erected that scorn-pole, as you recall. There I was, arse in the air, getting poked by a stallion with a cock the size of a frost-giant! I was so shamed that I had to leave Iceland."

"All right, all right. There, the money's in that bag. You're lucky I'm in a good mood, nephew. As it is, I have better things to think about than the pleasure of gutting Gisli. While you were gone, I was betrothed."

"Indeed?" I say, feigning interest. I pick up the bag, which isn't quite as bulge-full as when he offered it to me weeks ago. "To whom?"

"To Gisli's sister, Steingerd. She's a young beauty."

"What? By Odin! But she was your son's wife." *And young enough to be your daughter*, I want to blurt, but good judgment prevents me. "Does she know then, how you asked me to—?"

"She knows everything, poor lady. Gisli's actions horrified her, of course. Our mutual grief over Snorri's terrible end has brought us together. After what Gisli did, she wanted her brother dead as much as I."

I'm too stunned to continue the conversation and too eager to tell Gisli the shocking news. "Congratulations, uncle. And thank you," I mutter, heading for the door.

32.

As soon as I ride into Thorstein's garth, Patrick shambles toward me as quickly as his advanced age will allow.

"Sir! Thank Thor you're back. There's trouble. Your brother's found Gisli. He and the farmhands overpowered him."

Proof of Patrick's statement is immediately forthcoming. Thorstein and Gisli step out of the longhouse, along with three of my brother's men. Gisli's dressed in the hooded cloak old Helga sold us, and his hands are tethered in front of him.

"By Hel," I mutter, swinging down off my horse.

"Bound again," Gisli says with a satiric smile. "You Eiriksson brothers are over-fond of rope."

"What are you doing, brother?" I say.

"What are *you* doing, brother?" Thorstein says, jerking the wrist-tether so hard that Gisli falls to his knees. "Giving this killer of our kin refuge here? You told me he was dead."

I shrug my shoulders. "I lied. It was necessary."

"It was dishonorable. I'm going to take this man to Svein, as you should have."

"No, you aren't." I pat my sword-hilt. "While you've been keeping up the family farm, I've been overseas raiding and battling. Do you and your men really want to fight me?"

Thorstein's brow knits up. "No. No, we don't."

"Brother, you're always complaining about your debts, your lack of funds. I have a deal for you. You give me my friend there, and I give you this." I pull the bag of silver from my pouch. "I've booked passage on a ship. Tomorrow, Gisli and I are leaving Iceland."

"Why are you doing this, Einar? Are you mad? What is this scum to you? What about your duty?"

"I know my duty, Thorstein. Do you want this money or not?"

My brother rubs his cheek and scowls. "How…how much is it?"

"I don't know. Bring Gisli over here and you can count it."

Thorstein doesn't hesitate. He tugs Gisli to his feet and approaches, pulling Gisli behind him.

"There," I say, handing him the bag. "You can have all of that. I've already taken what I need."

Thorstein counts hurriedly. "By Odin," he sighs. "So much. This will save the farm."

"So that is sufficient? Will you give me my friend back?"

"All right," he snaps. Stepping back, he pushes Gisli forward. "It's a deal."

Gisli ambles over to stand by my side. "Well done," he mutters under his breath. "Now would you *please* untie me?"

"Later, perhaps," I whisper. "In return for a well-greased boon." I give him a quick grin before turning to my brother.

"Thorstein, know two things."

"Yes, Einar?" He's sifting through the coins with a rapt look on his face.

"First of all, freeing Gisli is just. He's innocent. That's all I'll say about that."

"Innocent? I doubt it. What else?"

"If you tell Svein that Gisli is still alive, he'll most likely take that money back."

Thorstein clutches the bag to him as if it were a precious infant in danger of being snatched away by a troll-wife. "I'll remember that."

"We leave tomorrow," I say. "May we stay here tonight?"

"By the gods, no. I'll not have—"

"Thorstein."

"Oh, fuck all. Yes! But not in the house. Stay in that shed you hid Gisli in. Just be out of here at dawn. I don't want Uncle Svein coming by for a visit before you've gone."

"I don't either." Especially if he's able to tear himself away from the courting of Steingerd long enough to consult Aunt Aud.

"Some supper later?" I call after him.

"Gods! Yes! I'll have some sent up." Thorstein slaps at the air and disappears inside.

"Come on, heart-thrall," I say, taking Gisli's wrist-tether and tugging him up the slope.

"You have me exactly where you want me, don't you?" Grinning, Gisli follows me toward the hut.

"Yes, indeed. We'll be many days at sea, and it's going to be sheer Hel to keep my hands off you for that long, so I plan on showering you with some rough use tonight."

33.

The wind is right, the day is fair, and the ship to Hamnavoe is nearly ready to depart. Gisli, still dressed in the hooded robe Helga sold us, is at the little market at the far end of the strand, purchasing some snacks for our journey.

I'm listening to the cry of the birds—gulls, curlews, and the *tjaldur*, that melancholy piping that always reminds me of Freysholm—when a woman's voice sounds behind me. "We'll miss you, nephew."

I turn, surprised. It's Aunt Aud, in her black priestess robes.

"If I were you, I'd get that Frey's-priest of yours hidden. My brother Svein is coming to the market today to deal with some traders. He'll probably be here any minute."

"Thor's hammer! Really? What are you doing here?"

"I'm here to see you off. You and your friend there."

She turns and beckons down the beach. Gisli's strolling toward us, carrying a bag heavy with purchases. His face is half-hidden by the hood, but still I can see his faint smile as he lifts his hand and waves.

"He's a handsome man," Aud says, her stern face softening. "He reminds me of a boy I knew in my youth. I can see why you care for him as you do."

"W-what do you mean?" I stammer, face flushing.

"I've had many the revelatory dream since you left, nephew. I've seen you shatter his sword. I've seen you leading him bound and silenced through lava fields and meadows. I've seen you in Frey's temple. I've seen you...well, let's just say that I've seen your fates intertwined, just as I predicted. Intertwined most sweatily."

"Aunt!" Now my face is burning like a long fire.

"The gods approve, even if men might not. You sought Gisli, and you found him. And now you are leaving. Off to Orkney?"

"Yes. His family hails from there. We hope to make a new life."

"You will, you will. I see a shattered sword reforged and many years shared happily. I see two gray-bearded warriors battling back to back. You will live together, and you will die together. Honorable deaths, protecting one another till the end."

"You have seen all that?"

"Yes. You two will have a better death than most. Better than Svein's, I think. Have you told Gisli about Steingerd's betrothal?"

"Yes. He's stunned. He told me that it was not he who murdered Snorri, but—"

"But Steingerd. Steingerd killed her husband. I know, nephew. As I said, I have had many visions since you left in search of Gisli. Steingerd slew the son, and now she's about to marry the father."

"Svein would slaughter her if he knew. Why did she agree to marry him?"

"Why do you think? Money. And money might lead her to slay another husband before she's done."

"Did she tell Gisli the truth? She said that Snorri raped their daughter. She claimed that was the reason she cut his throat."

"That I do not know. I only know my brother is besotted with her. She was as eager as he to see Gisli dead, no doubt hoping that the knowledge of her crime might die with him. You two do well to leave. And here's your friend now."

"Hello," Gisli says, loping up.

"Hello, Frey's-priest. I'm Einar's aunt."

"Svein's sister?" Gisli's face clouds.

"Yes. I'm here to give you my blessing. The gods have favored you, and they will do so for many years yet…as long as you two get on the ship now. My brother is just about to arrive, so go, go."

"Thank you, aunt. I hope to see you again one day."

"That will happen, I think," Aud says, grasping my hand. "In the prosperous house I see in your future, there will be room for guests. Now go."

There's Svein now, at the far end of the strand, dismounting before a merchant vessel. "Let's go, battle-brother," I say. With that, Gisli and I walk rapidly toward our ship.

34.

THERE THEY ARE, THE LAYERED rocks of Orkney. I stand behind Gisli on the spume-wet deck, breathing in the cool air and watching our destination loom closer.

"The Orkneys at last, my family's ancestral home. My dragon sword was created here. My father once said that Heart-Biter, if ever broken, could only be made whole again in the forge from whence it came," Gisli says. "And that forge is near here, on the isle of Rousay."

"Then we shall go there," I say, "and heal your sword in forge-flames, as your fire has healed me." I would take Gisli's hand, were there not so many sailors on deck.

Gisli is silent for a long time. Light glitters on the blue waters. "I'll never know if my sister told me the truth. Perhaps Snorri never ravished their child. Perhaps Steingerd killed Snorri so that she could marry into his father's money."

"Perhaps. Even Aud doesn't know what really happened. But I think Steingerd and Uncle Svein are a fine match. Two snakes in the same pit. I think the Norns have dark things planned for both of them."

"I fear that's true. Gods, Einar, could Steingerd have betrayed me?"

"Don't think of that, little man. Iceland's behind us. Orkney's ahead. And it looks beautiful."

"It does," Gisli says, gazing out toward the land. There's the town of Hamnavoe now, lining a harbor. "How will we live, Einar? That money of your uncle's won't last long."

"It's said that the earth is rich here. Perhaps it's time I left off raiding and put my energies into a farm. I'm no longer a rudderless wave-steed. My passions have an anchor now."

"Mine as well." Gisli gives me a happy grin. "Farming sounds fine. But won't we have trouble, two men living together?"

"Let's pass as brothers. No one knows us here."

"Or I could pretend to be your thrall. After all, I pledged my troth. You shattered my sword, and so I am your bondsman of a sort."

"How about you be my arse-thrall in bed, and my brother otherwise?"

"Yes, indeed." Gisli takes advantage of the rocking deck to stumble back against me, bumping my groin with his round rump. "Arse-thrall it is."

I give his butt a quick squeeze before resting a hand on his shoulder, pretending to steady him as the ship bucks beneath us. "Aud says we will have a long life together, and we will fall together in battle as old men."

"Yes? So be it. It sounds like *Wyrd* will be kind to us."

"Indeed. Once we've settled into this place, I want to pledge myself to you in the rite of *Fóstbróðir*."

Gisli turns, face flooded with light. "Blood-brotherhood? Truly?"

"Yes. I want to raise the strip of sod, open the flesh of our arms, and bind our wounds together. We are seed-brothers already, are we not, having each spent inside the other? Isn't it time we mingled our blood as well?"

"Thanks to Frey and Freya! Yes, Einar, yes," Gisli sighs. "It's time."

The ship bucks again, and Gisli stumbles back against me. He grabs my hand and squeezes it hard. Then we both step up to the rail as the vessel slides into the peaceful waters of Hamnavoe's sheltered harbor. Another few minutes, and, bags in hand, I follow my golden-bearded little man down the gangplank into a new land.

BIBLIOGRAPHY

Arnold, Martin. *Thor: Myth to Marvel* (Continuum International Publishing Group, 2011).

Barraclough, Eleanor Rosamund. *Beyond the Northlands: Viking Voyages and the Old Norse Sagas* (Oxford University Press, 2018).

"Battle of Stamford Bridge" (https://en.wikipedia.org/wiki/Battle_of_Stamford_Bridge).

Brogan, Stuart R. *Heathen Warrior: An Exploration into the Warrior Ethos within the Northern Tradition* (Midgard Books, 2013).

Brown, Nancy Marie. *The Real Valkyrie: The Hidden History of Viking Warrior Women* (St. Martin's Press, 2021).

---. *Song of the Vikings: Snorri and the Making of Norse Myths* (St. Martin's Griffin, 2014).

Brownworth, Lars. *The Sea Wolves: A History of the Vikings* (Crux Publishing, 2014).

Butler-Ehle, Hester. *Hearth and Field: A Heathen Prayer Book* (Fieldstone Hearth, 2011).

Byock, Jesse L., trans. *The Saga of King Hrolf Kraki* (Penguin Books, 1998).

---. *The Saga of the Volsungs* (Penguin Books, 1999).

Cook, Robert, trans. *Njal's Saga* (Penguin Books, 2001).

Crawford, Jackson, trans. *The Poetic Edda: Stories of the Norse Gods and Heroes* (Hackett Publishing Company, 2015).

---. *The Saga of the Volsungs with The Saga of Ragnar Lothbrok* (Hackett Publishing Company, 2017).

---. *Two Sagas of Mythical Heroes* (Hackett Publishing Company, 2021).

---. *The Wanderer's Hávamál* (Hackett Publishing Company, 2019).

Crossley-Holland, Kevin. *The Norse Myths* (Pantheon Books, 1980).

Davidson, H.R. Ellis. *Gods and Myths of Northern Europe* (Penguin Books, 1965).

Egerdahl, Kjersti. *The Viking Hondbók: Eat, Dress, and Fight Like a Warrior* (Running Press, 2020).

Fitch, Ed. *The Rites of Odin* (Llewellyn Publications, 1990).

Flowers, Stephen E. *Icelandic Magic: Practical Secrets of the Northern Grimoires* (Inner Traditions, 2016).

Fridriksdóttir, Jóhanna Katrín. *Valkyrie: The Women of the Viking World* (Bloomsbury, 2020.)

Gaiman, Neil. *Norse Mythology* (Norton, 2017).

Graham-Campbell, James. *The Viking World* (Frances Lincoln, 2013).

Hamilton, Edith. *Mythology: Timeless Tales of Gods and Heroes* (Grand Central Publishing, 2011).

Hasenfratz, Hans-Peter. *Barbarian Rites: The Spiritual World of the Vikings and the Germanic Tribes* (Inner Traditions, 2011).

Haywood, John. *The Penguin Historical Atlas of the Vikings* (Penguin Books, 1995).

---. *Viking: The Norse Warrior's (Unofficial) Manual* (Thames and Hudson, 2013).

Hollander, Lee M., trans. *The Poetic Edda* (University of Texas Press, 2001).

---. *Old Norse Poems* (Abela Publishing, 2010).

Hreinsson, Vidar, ed. *Comic Sagas and Tales from Iceland* (Penguin Books, 2013).

Hjardar, Kim, and Vegard Vike. *Vikings at War* (Casemate, 2019).

Jones, Gwyn. *Eirik the Red and Other Icelandic Sagas* (Oxford University Press, 2008).

Krasskova, Galina, and Raven Kaldera. *Northern Tradition for the Solitary Practitioner: A Book of Prayer, Devotional Practice, and the Nine Worlds of Spirit* (New Page Books/Weiser, 2009).

Kunz, Keneva, trans. *The Saga of the People of Laxardal and Bolli Bollason's Tale* (Penguin Books, 2008).

Larrington, Carolyne. *Norse Myths: A Guide to the Gods and Heroes* (Thames and Hudson, 2017).

---. *The Poetic Edda* (Oxford University Press, 2014).

Lindow, John. *Norse Mythology: A Guide to the Gods, Heroes, Rituals, and Beliefs* (Oxford University Press, 2002).

Magnusson, Magnus. *Iceland Saga* (Tempus Publishing, 2005).

McCoy, Daniel. *The Love of Destiny: The Sacred and the Profane in Germanic Polytheism* (CreateSpace Independent Publishing Platform, 2013).

---. *The Viking Spirit: An Introduction to Norse Mythology and Religion* (CreateSpace Independent Publishing Platform, 2016).

Metzner, Ralph. *The Well of Remembrance: Rediscovering the Earth Wisdom Myths of Northern Europe* (Shambhala Publications, 1994).

Moore, Robert, and Douglas Gillette. *King, Warrior, Magician, Lover: Rediscovering the Archetypes of the Mature Masculine* (HarperOne, 1991).

Mountfort, Paul Rhys. *Nordic Runes: Understanding, Casting, and Interpreting the Ancient Viking Oracle* (Destiny Books, 2003).

O'Connor, Ralph, trans. *Icelandic Histories and Romances* (The History Press, 2006).

Odinsson, Eoghan. *Northern Wisdom: The Havamal, Tao of the Vikings* (Asgard Studios, 2012).

O'Donoghue, Heather. *From Asgard to Valhalla: The Remarkable History of the Norse Myths* (I.B. Tauris, 2013).

Ólason, Vésteinn, intro. *Gisli Sursson's Saga and The Saga of the People of Eyri* (Penguin Books, 2003).

Overing, Gillian R., and Marijane Osborn. *Landscape of Desire: Partial Stories of the Medieval Scandinavian World* (University of Minnesota Press, 1994).

Pálsson, Hermann, trans. *Hrafnkel's Saga and Other Stories* (Penguin Books, 1971).

Pálsson, Hermann, and Paul Edwards, trans. *Eyrbyggja Saga* (Penguin Books, 1989).

---. *Orkneyinga Saga: The History of the Earls of Orkney* (Penguin Books, 1981).

---. *Seven Viking Romances* (Penguin Books, 1985).

Paxson, Diana L. *Essential Asatru: A Modern Guide to Norse Paganism* (Citadel, 2021).

---. *Odin: Ecstasy, Runes & Norse Magic* (Weiser Books, 2017).

---. *Taking Up the Runes: A Complete Guide to Using Runes in Spells, Rituals, Divination, and Magic* (Weiser Books, 2005).

Price, Neil. *Children of Ash and Elm: A History of the Vikings* (Basic Books, 2020).

Scudder, Bernard, trans. *Egil's Saga* (Penguin Books, 2004).

---. *The Saga of Grettir the Strong* (Penguin Books, 2005).

Sheffield, Ann Gróa. *Frey: God of the World* (Lulu.com, 2007).

Shippey, Tom. *Laughing Shall I Die: Lives and Deaths of the Great Vikings* (Reaktion Books, 2018).

Short, William R. *Icelanders in the Viking Age: The People of the Sagas* (McFarland and Company, 2010).

---. *Viking Weapons and Combat Techniques* (Westholme Publishing, 2014).

Short, William R., and Reynir A. Oskarson. *Men of Terror: A Comprehensive Analysis of Viking Combat* (Westholme Publishing, 2021).

Skallagrimsson, Weyland. *Odin's Way in the Modern World* (CreateSpace Independent Publishing Platform, 2013).

Smiley, Jane, and Robert Kellogg. *The Sagas of Icelanders* (Penguin Classics, 2001).

Sturluson, Snorri. *Edda* (Everyman, 2002).

Thorsson, Edred. *A Book of Troth* (Runestone Press, 2015).

---. *Futhark: A Handbook of Rune Magic* (Weiser Books, 1984).

Waggoner, Ben, trans. *Hávamál: A New Translation* (Troth Publications, 2017).

---. *The Hrafnista Sagas* (Troth Publications, 2012).

---. *A Pocket Guide to Runes* (Troth Publications, 2019).

---. *The Sagas of Fridthjof the Bold* (2009).

---. *Sagas of Giants and Heroes* (Troth Publications, 2010).

---. *The Sagas of Ragnar Lodbrok* (Troth Publications, 2009).

Whaley, Diana, intro. *Sagas of Warrior-Poets* (Penguin Books, 2002).

Williams, Gareth. *The Viking Ship* (The British Museum Press, 2014).

Winroth, Anders. *The Age of the Vikings* (Princeton University Press, 2014).

ABOUT THE AUTHOR

JEFF MANN grew up in Covington, Virginia, and Hinton, West Virginia, receiving degrees in English and forestry from West Virginia University. His poetry, fiction, and essays have appeared in many publications, including *Arts and Letters, Prairie Schooner, Shenandoah, Willow Springs, The Gay and Lesbian Review Worldwide, Crab Orchard Review,* and *Appalachian Heritage.* He has published three award-winning poetry chapbooks, *Bliss, Mountain Fireflies,* and *Flint Shards from Sussex;* six full-length books of poetry, *Bones Washed with Wine, On the Tongue, Ash: Poems from Norse Mythology, A Romantic Mann, Rebels,* and *Redneck Bouquet;* three collections of personal essays, *Edge: Travels of an Appalachian Leather Bear, Binding the God: Ursine Essays from the Mountain South,* and *Endangered Species: A Surly Bear in the Bible Belt;* three novellas, *Devoured,* included in *Masters of Midnight: Erotic Tales of the Vampire, Camp Allegheny,* included in *History's Passion: Stories of Sex Before Stonewall,* and *The Saga of Einar and Gisli,* included in *On the Run: Tales of Gay Pursuit and Passion;* six novels, *Cub, Country, Insatiable, Fog: A Novel of Desire and Reprisal* (which won the Pauline Réage Novel Award), *Purgatory: A Novel of the Civil War* (which won a Rainbow Award), and *Salvation: A Novel of the Civil War* (which won both the Pauline Réage Novel Award and a Lambda Literary Award); a book of poetry and memoir, *Loving Mountains, Loving Men;* and three volumes of short fiction, *Desire and Devour: Stories of Blood and Sweat, Consent: Bondage Tales,* and *A History of Barbed Wire* (which won a Lambda Literary Award). With Julia Watts, he co-edited *LGBTQ Fiction and Poetry from Appalachia.* In 2013, he was inducted into the Saints and Sinners Literary Festival Hall of Fame. He teaches creative writing at Virginia Tech in Blacksburg, Virginia.